THE ORPHAN ANGEL'S GRACE

DOROTHY WELLINGS

CORNERSTONETALES.COM

1

THE LAMP LIGHTER

The gas lamps of Whitechapel stood like sentinels along the narrow, winding streets, waiting for William Hartwell's touch to bring them to life. As twilight descended, the first wisps of London fog began their slow dance, curling around corners and softening the hard edges of the weathered buildings. Grace watched from the doorway of their rooms above Grigson's Bakery, her breath forming small clouds in the cooling air.

"Are you ready, my little lamplight?" Her Father called, adjusting the worn leather strap of his tool bag across his broad shoulders.

Grace nodded eagerly, tying back her fiery red hair with a faded ribbon. She loved these evenings more than anything—walking London's labyrinthine streets beside her father, learning the secret geography of their city as he brought light to darkness.

Down below, children darted between market stalls, their laughter rising above the chorus of vendors hawking their wares. "Fresh bread, still warm! Penny trinkets for the little ones!" The calls melded together into the familiar symphony of Whitechapel at dusk.

Her Father checked his equipment with practiced hands—the long lighting pole with its small flame cup at the end, the sturdy lantern hook for adjustments, and the small pouch of matches. His movements were deliberate, a ritual Grace had watched countless times.

"We'd best have something in our bellies before we set out," he said, gesturing to their small table where the last of the morning's bread waited.

The warm, yeasty aroma of the bakery below had permeated their rooms all day, making Grace's stomach rumble in anticipation. Mr Grigson often slipped them day-old loaves that couldn't be sold—a kindness that meant they rarely went without.

"You have the last piece, Father." Grace pushed the slightly larger portion toward him, her green eyes earnest.

His weathered face creased into a smile. "Always thinking of others, just like your mother." He broke the piece in half instead. "We'll share it properly."

When they stepped outside, the chill evening air nipped at Grace's cheeks, a sharp contrast to their warm rooms. The Thames carried its peculiar scent—earthy and ancient—mingling with the sweeter notes of baking bread and roasting chestnuts from a nearby vendor.

"Stay close now," her Father reminded, his hand gentle on her shoulder as they navigated the crowded street. "Evening, Mrs Finch! How's that grandson of yours?" he called to an elderly woman arranging knitted scarves on a makeshift table.

"Growing like a weed, William! And your Grace gets prettier every day—the very image of Mary, God rest her soul."

Grace felt the familiar warmth of pride at being compared to the mother she'd never known. She matched her father's steady pace, her smaller feet finding the rhythm of his steps across the uneven cobblestones.

"Hello, Mr Hartwell!" A group of small children waved enthusiastically from a doorway.

"Evening, little ones. Mind you are home before full dark now." Father always had time for the children, often slipping them bits of candy from his pocket.

Grace memorised each turn they took, each shop they passed. She knew which corners collected puddles after rain, which doorways offered shelter during sudden downpours. She recognised faces—the butcher closing his shop, the seamstress hurrying home with bundles of mending, the elderly man who fed stray cats behind the chandler's.

"This is our kingdom," her Father often told her, "and we bring the stars to earth each night."

As they approached the first lamp, he readied his pole, and Grace stepped back to watch the magic begin—the moment when her father would transform from an ordinary man to bringer of light.

With practiced precision, her father extended his long pole towards the first gas lamp. Grace watched, transfixed, as the small flame at the pole's end touched the lamp's wick. For a heartbeat, nothing happened—then a soft whoosh as golden light bloomed above them, pushing back the gathering shadows.

"There she goes," he murmured with satisfaction.

The lamplight cast a warm glow across the faces of weary workers trudging home after long days in factories and workshops. Tired expressions softened as they passed through the circle of light, nodding gratefully to William.

"Evening, Hartwell. God bless you for your work."

Grace observed how the simple act transformed the street —not just physically illuminating the cobblestones and brick facades, but somehow lifting the spirits of those who passed through its radiance.

"Each lamp we light is more than just fire and gas, Grace," her father explained as they moved to the next post. "Before the lamps, these streets were dangerous places after dark. Thieves and footpads lurked in shadows, waiting to prey on honest folk."

He reached up with his pole again, and another lamp flickered to life.

"Your grandfather remembered when they first installed these beauties. Changed everything, he said. Not just safer streets, but people could work longer hours, shops stayed open later. The light brought life."

As they continued their rounds, William's stories shifted from lamp lighting to memories of Mary. Grace drank in every word, constructing the image of her mother from these precious fragments.

"Your mother had the most beautiful singing voice," her father said, his eyes crinkling at the corners. "She'd sing hymns while mixing her remedies—said the music made the medicine stronger. The neighbours would open their windows just to hear her."

Grace tried to imagine it—her mother's hands working with herbs while her voice lifted in song. Though she'd never heard it, she felt certain her mother's voice must have been as warm as the lamplight surrounding them.

"She knew just which plants to use for every ailment. When old Mr Barton's chest infection wouldn't clear, the doctor had given up hope. But your mother made a special tea with thyme and honey that had him breathing easier by morning."

Her father paused beneath a newly lit lamp and reached inside his coat. From an inner pocket, he withdrew a small golden locket. Opening it carefully, he held it out for Grace to see.

"Here she is, my love."

Grace gazed at the tiny portrait—a young woman with fiery hair like her own, green eyes sparkling with life, her smile both gentle and mischievous.

"She's beautiful," Grace whispered, her heart aching with longing.

"And you grow more like her every day."

Grace began to hum softly—one of the hymns her father had taught her, explaining it was Mary's favourite. Her father's voice caught as he joined in, their melody rising into the evening air.

They approached the small cottage of Mrs O'Malley, an elderly widow whose husband had been a lamplighter alongside her father years ago. The old woman sat on her doorstep, wincing as she tried to adjust her position.

"Evening, Mrs O'Malley. Troubling you again, is it?" he called.

"This ankle's giving me grief something terrible," she replied, her weathered face pinched with pain.

Grace stepped forward. "May I help?" She knelt beside the old woman, gently examining the swollen joint. "Father, do you think we could make a poultice like the one Mother used for sprains? With comfrey and arnica?"

Her father nodded approvingly. "We have those dried at home."

"Your mother saved my Thomas when he fell from the ladder," Mrs O'Malley said, patting Grace's hand. "Had him back on his feet in three days when the doctor said it would be weeks. You've got her touch, child."

Grace felt a flush of pride warm her cheeks. "We'll bring the poultice tomorrow morning," she promised.

As they continued their rounds, they passed a small patch of wildflowers growing between cobblestones. Grace paused, bending to examine them.

"Father, isn't this yarrow? Mother used it for fevers, didn't she?"

He smiled. "That's right. You've a good eye for it."

"I want to learn all of Mother's remedies," Grace said earnestly. "To help people the way she did."

"Nothing would make her prouder," her father replied.

Later, they paused in a quiet square where moonlight filtered through the branches of an old oak tree. Her father produced her mother's worn prayer book from his coat pocket.

"Would you read tonight's passage, Grace?"

She took the book reverently, finding the marked page. Her clear voice rose in the stillness, reciting words of comfort and hope. Though the night grew chilly around them, Grace felt warm—connected to her mother through these shared words, through the healing knowledge passed down, through the light they brought to dark places.

With the last lamp flickering to life on their route, the two of them turned towards home. The bakery's chimney puffed welcoming smoke against the darkened sky as they approached, their footsteps echoing on the cobblestones. The day's labours had left them tired but content, the satisfaction of completed duty warming them against the evening chill.

Their small room greeted them with modest comfort—the single window overlooking the street below, the worn rug Grace had painstakingly cleaned last week, the kettle waiting patiently on the small stove. Her father stoked the fire while Grace hung their coats on pegs by the door.

"Come, let me show you something useful," he said, retrieving his work shirt from a basket. He held it up, revealing a tear along the seam. "A lamplighter needs steady hands for more than just lighting."

Grace settled beside him at their table, watching intently as his weathered fingers demonstrated the careful back-and-forth motion of needle and thread.

"Small stitches, close together," he instructed, guiding her hand. "Your mother could mend anything—said there was dignity in keeping things whole."

Grace's tongue poked between her teeth as she concentrated, her stitches gradually becoming more even. "Was Mother good at everything?"

Her father chuckled. "Not everything. She couldn't carry a tune in a bucket when we first met. But she practiced singing hymns every day because she believed they brought comfort to the sick."

The shirt mended, Grace moved to prepare their supper. She stirred the pot of porridge bubbling on the stove, adding a precious pinch of cinnamon—a rare treat Mr Grigson had given them.

"Your mother always said food made with love tasted better," her father remarked, setting out their bowls. "She'd add herbs not just for health but for happiness too. Said a sprig of mint could lift the heaviest heart."

They ate by lamplight, her father sharing tales of mother tending to neighbours during a difficult winter, mixing tonics and singing softly to feverish children. Grace absorbed every word, building the mosaic of her mother piece by precious piece.

After supper, Grace settled on her small bed, journal open on her lap. She carefully sketched the yarrow they'd found, noting its feathery leaves and tiny flowers. Beside the drawing, she wrote: "Good for fevers and wounds. Mother used it often."

Her father approached, and smoothed her hair.

"Remember, little lamplight, no matter what challenges come, our love and faith will guide us. Just as we bring light to dark streets, so does God's love illuminate our path."

Grace nestled beneath her blanket, listening to the comforting sounds of her father preparing for bed and the distant hum of the bakery below. Tomorrow would bring new lessons, new herbs to discover, new people to help. Her eyes grew heavy, dreams of healing hands and glowing lamps mingling as she drifted off, safe in the knowledge that she was loved—by her father beside her and her mother watching from above.

2

THE FOG

The fog crept through London like a living thing, slithering between buildings and swallowing whole streets. Grace watched it from their small window, her breath fogging the glass as the grey mass thickened with each passing minute. The warm, yeasty smell of Mr Grigson's evening baking wafted up through the floorboards, a comforting contrast to the eerie silence settling outside.

"It's getting worse, Papa," she whispered, turning to where her father stood adjusting his coat buttons.

Her father moved to join her at the window, his weathered face reflected in the glass. His eyes narrowed at the sight of the infamous "pea-souper" that had descended upon the city, transforming familiar streets into an unknowable landscape. Even the nearest lamppost was barely visible, its glow reduced to a faint, ghostly orb in the murk.

"I've not seen one this thick in years," he admitted, reaching for his lamplighter's pole propped against the wall. "But the lamps won't light themselves."

Grace's stomach tightened with dread. At twelve, she was

old enough to understand the dangers that lurked in London's fog—carriages unable to see pedestrians, people losing their way mere steps from their own doors, the Thames a silent, deadly trap for the disoriented.

"You can't go out tonight," she protested, moving to block the door. "Mr Grigson said three men fell into the canal last month during a fog half this thick!"

William gathered his tools methodically, his movements betraying no hesitation. "The city needs its light most on nights like this, Grace. That's what being a lamplighter means."

Grace clutched his arm as he reached for the door handle, her fingers digging into the rough wool of his coat. "Please, Papa! It's too thick, you can't see! Don't go!" Her voice cracked, fear making her sound younger than her years.

Her father paused, setting down his pole to place both hands on her shoulders. His eyes, the same deep green as her own, softened as they met her worried gaze.

"I've weathered worse, love. The city depends on me." His tone was gentle but firm, the same voice he used when teaching her important lessons about responsibility and duty.

Grace saw the flicker of concern in his eyes that he tried to hide. Her father, always so solid and certain, wasn't as confident as he pretended. The knowledge only intensified her fear.

He hoisted his pole, the familiar tool looking suddenly inadequate against the monstrous fog. With a final reassuring smile that didn't quite reach his eyes, He stepped out into the swirling grey. The door closed behind him with a soft click.

Grace pressed her face against the window once more, watching her father's form dissolve into the fog. The lantern he carried glowed faintly, a small star being steadily extinguished by the relentless mist. The sound of his footsteps faded quickly, muffled by the thick air until all she could hear was the distant clanging of the bakery pans below and her own shallow breathing.

"Please come back," she whispered against the cold glass, her words creating small clouds that disappeared as quickly as her father had.

3
LOST

Three days had passed since the fog swallowed her father whole. Three days of Grace peering out the window at every sound, praying to glimpse his familiar silhouette emerging from the mist. Three days of Mr Grigson's increasingly worried glances as he brought up trays of bread and soup that went mostly untouched.

On the morning of the fourth day, the fog finally lifted enough to reveal a watery sun. Grace had just begun to hope when heavy footsteps trudged up the stairs to their rooms. Mr Grigson's round face appeared, ashen and drawn, his baker's cap twisted between flour-dusted fingers.

"Miss Grace," he began, his voice cracking. "They found him, love. Down by the river."

The words hung in the air between them, monstrous and impossible.

"No," Grace whispered, backing away. "He's just lost his way. The fog—"

Mr Grigson shook his head, tears welling in his kind eyes. "The dockworkers spotted him this morning. Caught in the debris near Wapping. Still ... still holding his lantern, he was."

Grace's legs gave way beneath her. She crumpled onto the wooden chair by the window—her father's chair—where he'd sat mending her stockings just three nights before. The room tilted sickeningly around her.

"They're bringing him to the parish house," Mr Grigson continued softly. "I'll take you when you're ready."

When he left, Grace sat motionless, her breath coming in shallow gasps. The small room suddenly seemed vast and empty, echoing with absences. Her gaze fell on her father's nightshirt, still draped over the bed rail, waiting for his return. His boots stood by the door, perfectly aligned as always.

She reached for her mother's prayer book, kept safely on the shelf beside her bed. She clutched it to her chest, breathing in its familiar scent of age and lavender.

"And the light shineth in darkness," she whispered, reciting her mother's favourite passage, "and the darkness comprehended it not."

But the darkness had comprehended. It had reached out with greedy fingers and taken her father, just as surely as illness had claimed her mother years before.

Memories rushed at her like a tide—her father's voice spinning tales of her mother's healing gifts, his patient hands showing her how to mend a tear, the warmth of his embrace after a nightmare. The weight of his absence crashed down upon her, stealing her breath.

Grace touched the small locket around her neck—her mother's portrait inside, her father's most precious gift to her. It felt impossibly heavy now, a burden rather than a comfort. She was truly alone.

Outside, she could hear the murmurs spreading through Whitechapel like wildfire. "The lamplighter," they whispered.

"Found with his lantern still clutched in his hand." The neighbours who had waved to him each evening, the children who had followed him on his rounds, all sharing the news with hushed voices and damp eyes.

In the bakery below, customers gathered, their voices rising and falling in sorrowful waves. "Such a good man," they said. "And the poor child, all alone now."

All alone. The words echoed in Grace's mind as she sat motionless, the prayer book pressed against her heart, watching the sun break through the last wisps of the murderous fog.

4

LIGHT IN THE DARKNESS

A week after her father's simple burial, Mr Grigson knocked gently on Grace's door. The small gathering at the cemetery had dispersed quickly, leaving only wet earth and a wooden marker to show where William Hartwell now rested. Grace hadn't cried since that day—her tears seemed locked away somewhere unreachable.

"Might I have a word, lass?" Mr Grigson asked, settling his bulky frame onto the three-legged stool by the hearth.

Grace nodded, her hands busy sorting through her father's meagre belongings—a spare shirt, his Sunday boots, a few small documents scrawled in an almost unreadable hand. Each item felt sacred now, imbued with memories of his touch.

Mr Grigson removed his flour-dusted cap, twisting it between thick fingers. His face, usually ruddy and cheerful, looked pale and drawn. "You know I think the world of you, Grace. Your father was the finest man I knew."

"Thank you, sir," Grace murmured, already sensing what was coming.

"The thing is," he continued, his voice catching, "business

ain't what it was. The mill's raised flour prices again, and folks can barely afford a half-loaf these days." He gestured helplessly at the cramped room. "I can offer you a roof for a few nights more, but my situation is dire, lass. I can't feed you forever."

Grace looked up from the small pile of her father's things. Mr Grigson's eyes shimmered with unshed tears, his broad shoulders slumped with the weight of his words.

"You've been more than kind," she said softly. "Father always spoke highly of you."

"He was a good man, your da." Mr Grigson reached out, his calloused hand covering her small one. "I've asked around about work for you. Mrs Tanner might need help with laundry. It ain't much, but—"

"I understand." Grace's fingers closed around her father's lamplighter's badge, the metal cool against her palm. She'd found it tucked inside his jacket pocket, somehow still gleaming despite its journey in the Thames.

After Mr Grigson left, Grace moved to the small window overlooking Whitechapel Road. Below, London continued its relentless pace—carts rattling over cobblestones, vendors hawking wares, children darting between hurried adults. None glanced up at the small girl watching from above, none aware that her world had collapsed into this tiny room with its dwindling supply of coal and hope.

"What would you do, Father?" she whispered, pressing her forehead against the cold glass.

His voice seemed to answer from memory: "When darkness falls, Grace, we bring the light. That's our duty."

She clutched the badge tighter, feeling its edges press into her flesh. Her father had taught her more than prayers and remedies—he'd shown her how to face each day with dignity and purpose, how to find kindness even in London's meanest streets.

Grace moved to the small table where she'd laid out her few possessions—her mother's prayer book, the locket with Mary's portrait, a small bundle of dried yarrow she'd collected on their last walk together. Beside them, she placed her father's badge.

"I will find a way," she whispered, straightening her shoulders as the first light of morning crept through the window. "I promise."

She thought of Mrs O'Malley, whose ankle had healed thanks to Grace's poultice. Of old Mr Finch, who'd always had a peppermint stick for her when she accompanied her father on his rounds. Of the community that had respected William Hartwell for his unfailing service.

As London stirred to life outside, Grace began to formulate a plan. Her father had believed in the fundamental goodness of people. Perhaps that goodness would extend to his orphaned daughter, if she was brave enough to ask.

5
DISTANT COUSINS

Grace sat cross-legged on the floor beside her bed, the fading twilight casting long shadows across the familiar contours of her small room. A stub of candle flickered beside her as she scribbled in a worn journal—notes about yarrow poultices, feverfew teas, and other remedies her father had passed down from her mother. Her handwriting was neat but cramped, desperate to capture every detail before memory faded.

"Making good use of that journal, I see."

Mr Grigson stood in the doorway, his frame blocking what little light remained from the corridor.

"Yes, sir." Grace closed the book carefully. "I'm writing Mother's remedies, so I won't forget."

Mr Grigson's face softened as he stepped into the room, lowering himself onto the three-legged stool with a groan. "I've news, lass. Been asking around about your family. Turns out your father had relatives—distant cousins in Bermondsey."

Grace's heart stuttered. "Relatives? Father never mentioned—"

"Might not have known himself. But I've sent word, and they've agreed to take you in." He attempted a smile that didn't quite reach his eyes. "Proper family, they are. Clerk for an insurance firm. Wife and two children. Better environment than a workhouse, that's certain."

The words fell heavy between them. Grace clutched her mother's locket hanging from her neck, her thumb tracing its familiar contours. "When must I go?"

"Tomorrow morning." Mr Grigson twisted his cap between flour-dusted fingers. "I'd keep you if I could, Grace. You know that."

Grace nodded, unable to speak past the lump in her throat. She'd known this moment was coming, yet the reality of leaving the only home she'd ever known stabbed sharper than expected.

"I'll leave you to pack your things." Mr Grigson rose with difficulty, his knees cracking. At the door, he paused. "Your father would want you with family. It's for the best."

After he left, Grace sat motionless in the growing darkness. Family. The word felt hollow. Her family lay in fresh-turned earth beside her mother's grave. These cousins were strangers.

With trembling hands, she reached for her mother's prayer book, opening to the inscription inside: "To Mary, my light in darkness. With eternal love, William." The familiar words blurred as tears finally came, hot and silent.

When dawn broke, Grace had packed their few belongings into a small cloth bundle—the warped wooden horse her father had carved for her sixth birthday, a chipped teacup her mother had treasured, the prayer book, and her journal of remedies. Her clothing barely filled half the bundle.

She stood at the window, watching as lamplighters extinguished the morning gas lamps. In her mind's eye, she saw her father's face glowing in the warm light as he performed his duties, pole extended upward in a practiced motion.

"I won't forget," she whispered, pressing her palm against the cool glass. "I promise."

Mr Grigson waited below, his cart loaded with flour sacks. He'd offered to take her to Bermondsey on his delivery rounds. Grace took one last look at the small room—the sagging bed where her father had told her stories, the hearth where they'd shared simple meals, the corner where he'd taught her to mend and pray.

She closed the door softly behind her, each step down the narrow stairs taking her further from everything familiar and into a future she couldn't imagine.

"Ready, lass?" Mr Grigson asked, offering his hand to help her onto the cart.

Grace clutched her bundle tighter, feeling the hard outline of her father's lamplighter badge wrapped within. "Yes, sir," she lied, and climbed aboard.

6

A NEW HOME

The cart rattled through London's winding streets, Grace holding tight to her bundle as Mr Grigson navigated the busy thoroughfares. They crossed the river at London Bridge, leaving behind the familiar streets of Whitechapel for the unknown territory of Bermondsey. With each clop of the horse's hooves, Grace felt the distance growing between herself and everything she had known.

"There it is," Mr Grigson announced, pointing his whip toward a row of terraced houses on a quiet street. "Hartwell residence."

Grace studied the house with wary eyes. It stood slightly larger than her former home above the bakery, with a modest garden at the front—a few scraggly rosebushes and an iron gate that suggested prosperity beyond what she had known. The bricks were cleaner, the windows larger, and the curtains within pressed and proper.

Mr Grigson helped her down from the cart and approached the door, rapping three times with weathered knuckles. The door swung open to reveal a tall, thin man with receding dark hair and a perpetual frown etched between his brows.

"Mr Hartwell? I'm Thomas Grigson, the baker who wrote to you." He gestured toward Grace. "This is Grace, William's daughter."

Cornelius Hartwell's mouth formed a stiff, formal smile. "Yes, of course. The orphan." He studied Grace with detached curiosity, as though examining an unusual specimen.

A woman appeared behind him. Agatha Hartwell was cold-looking with greying hair pulled severely back from her face, her eyes narrowed as they swept over Grace's worn dress and small bundle.

"So this is her, then?" Agatha's tone suggested disappointment with what she saw.

"She's a good girl," Mr Grigson said, placing a gentle hand on Grace's shoulder. "Smart as a whip and handy with remedies, just like her mother was."

Two children suddenly burst through the gap between the adults, racing outside with shrieks of laughter. The boy, no more than eight, shoved the older girl, who retaliated by tugging his collar. Both wore clothes finer than anything Grace had owned—polished shoes and fabrics without patches or visible mending.

They paused momentarily to stare at Grace, their expressions mixing innocent curiosity with unmistakable disdain, before resuming their game and disappearing around the side of the house.

"Violet! Humphrey! Mind your manners!" Agatha called after them, though her reprimand lacked conviction.

Mr Grigson cleared his throat. "Well then, I'll leave you to get acquainted." He turned to Grace, his eyes softening. "You take care now, lass."

Before Grace could respond, he was climbing back onto his

cart, leaving her alone with these strangers who shared her name but nothing of her heart.

"Come inside," Agatha commanded, her tone curt as she ushered Grace through the doorway. "No sense standing about for the neighbours to gawk."

The living room beyond was cluttered with evidence of family life—toys scattered across the floor, half-finished needlework on a chair, papers piled on side tables. It lacked the simple orderliness of the bakery rooms Grace had kept tidy for her father.

"That corner will be your space," Agatha pointed to a small area beside the hearth, barely large enough for Grace's bundle. "You'll sleep upstairs in the attic. I've put a mattress there."

Cornelius retreated to his office, hastily resuming his clerical work, quill scratching against parchment as though Grace's arrival were a mere interruption to his important tasks.

"We run things differently here," Agatha continued, arms crossed over her chest. "Everyone contributes, especially those who arrive unexpectedly. You'll help with the cooking, cleaning, mending, and looking after Violet and Humphrey. It's only fair you earn your keep, considering the burden—" She caught herself. "Considering the circumstances."

Violet darted past Grace, clutching a porcelain doll with golden curls and a lace-trimmed dress. She thrust it before Grace's face, twirling it so the tiny skirts flared out.

"Father brought her from the city. She's French," Violet announced, her voice rising with importance. "She cost more than your entire bundle, I expect."

Grace's fingers tightened around her own small package of belongings. She nodded politely, trying to recall her father's lessons about kindness even when it wasn't returned.

"She's very pretty," Grace offered, reaching out to touch the doll's delicate sleeve.

Violet yanked the toy away. "Don't! Your hands are dirty from the cart." She inspected the doll for imaginary marks. "Mama says street children carry all sorts of filth."

"I'm not a street child," Grace replied softly. "I lived above Mr Grigson's bakery."

"Same thing," Violet sniffed, turning the doll away as though to shield it from contamination.

A sharp tug at Grace's hair sent pain shooting across her scalp. She spun around to find Humphrey giggling, a strand of her auburn hair wrapped around his pudgy finger.

"It's red like fire!" he shrieked with delight. "Does it burn when I pull it?"

He yanked again, harder this time. Grace bit her lip to keep from crying out.

"Humphrey, that's enough," Cornelius muttered as he passed through the hallway, though he didn't look up from his papers in his hands.

The boy ignored his father, giving another experimental tug. "Why'd you come here? We didn't ask for you."

Grace gently unwound her hair from his grasp. "I'm your cousin. My father—"

"Your father fell in the river," Humphrey interrupted, his voice sing-song with mockery. "Violet says only drunks fall in the river."

"Humphrey!" Agatha's voice held warning, but not for the cruelty—only for speaking of such matters aloud.

Grace swallowed the lump forming in her throat. Her father had never touched a drop of spirits; it was the fog that had claimed him, not drink. But she wouldn't give them the satisfaction of seeing her cry.

"May I see where I'll be sleeping?" she asked quietly.

Agatha sighed as though the request were an imposition.

"Violet, show her the attic stairs. Then both of you wash for supper. I won't have dirty hands at my table."

Violet led Grace through a narrow corridor to a steep staircase tucked behind the kitchen. "Up there," she said, pointing to the dark opening above. "Mind the steps—they creak something awful."

Grace climbed slowly, each wooden stair groaning beneath her weight. The attic was low-ceilinged and stifling, dust motes dancing in the thin light from a single small window. A straw mattress lay in the corner, threadbare blanket folded atop it.

This was to be her home now.

Grace placed her bundle carefully on the mattress, unwrapping it just enough to touch her father's lamplighter badge for courage. She would make this work. She would be useful, indispensable even. She would earn their respect, perhaps one day even their affection.

Downstairs, Agatha's voice rang out sharp and impatient: "Grace! Don't dawdle! There's potatoes to be peeled!"

Grace tucked the badge away and straightened her shoulders. Her father had taught her that even on the darkest nights, a lamplighter's duty was to bring light. She would find a way to shine here, despite the shadows gathering around her.

"Coming, Mrs Hartwell," she called, descending the creaking stairs to face whatever tasks awaited.

7
A COLD HOME

"Grace! Where are the potatoes? I told you to peel them, not stand there daydreaming!" Agatha's voice cut through the kitchen like a knife.

Grace startled from her thoughts and hurried to the small basket of potatoes sitting on the worn wooden table. She hadn't been daydreaming at all—merely taking a moment to collect herself after the whirlwind of arriving at this cold new home.

"Yes, Mrs Hartwell," she murmured, picking up the dull knife left beside the basket.

Agatha bustled about, yanking open cupboards and slamming them shut. "When you've finished with those, there's carrots to chop and the table to set. The silver needs polishing too—not that I expect you to know how to handle proper cutlery."

Grace worked swiftly, her fingers soon stained brown from the potato skins. She'd helped her father prepare meals countless times in their small room above the bakery. Though they'd had little, those simple suppers had been filled with stories and laughter. Here, the kitchen felt vast and hollow despite Agatha's constant presence.

"Mind you don't waste any—scrape them thin," Agatha instructed, hovering over Grace's shoulder. "And don't cut yourself. I'll not have blood on my food."

From the parlour came peals of laughter. Violet's high-pitched giggles mingled with Humphrey's deeper chortles as they played some game together. The sound pierced Grace's heart like a thorn. Just days ago, she'd sat beside her father, listening to his gentle voice as he read from her mother's prayer book. Now she stood alone in a strange kitchen, surrounded by people who saw her as nothing more than an unwelcome burden.

"What's taking so long? The potatoes should be in the pot by now!" Agatha snapped, returning from checking on her children.

Grace worked faster, her knuckles white around the knife handle. "Nearly done, Mrs Hartwell."

Another burst of laughter erupted from the parlour, followed by Violet's excited voice: "Papa, look what Humphrey made!"

Cornelius's deep chuckle joined the children's merriment. Grace bit her lip, focusing intently on the task before her. She would not cry. She would not let them see her weakness.

When the potatoes were finally peeled and boiling, Agatha thrust a rag and tin of polish into Grace's hands. "The silver now. Every piece must shine."

Grace nodded, taking the items to the dining table. It was already set with fine china plates and crystal glasses that caught the fading afternoon light. Such luxury compared to the chipped teacup she'd carefully wrapped in her bundle upstairs.

As she polished each fork and knife, Grace watched the family through the doorway. They sat together in the parlour,

Violet showing off her doll's new dress while Humphrey built something with wooden blocks. Cornelius looked on with mild interest, occasionally patting one child's head or commenting on their activities. Agatha moved between them, straightening Violet's hair ribbon or adjusting Humphrey's collar.

They were a family—imperfect perhaps, but whole. And Grace stood outside their circle, as invisible as if she were still trapped in London's fog.

She rubbed the silver harder, channeling her hurt into determination. Each piece began to gleam under her persistent efforts. Perhaps that was all she could do for now—polish what was tarnished, mend what was torn, and make herself useful enough that they might one day see her as more than just "the orphan."

The laughter continued, never including her, but Grace worked on, one piece of silver at a time.

GRACE CLIMBED the narrow staircase to the attic, each creaking step a reminder of her new station in life. Her arms ached from scrubbing pots, her back sore from stooping over the hearth. The meagre portion of stew she'd been allowed—after the family had taken their fill—sat like a stone in her empty stomach.

The attic room was frigid, moonlight spilling through the small dormer window onto the thin mattress that served as her bed. Grace sank down onto the floor beside the window, tears pooling in her eyes as she gazed out at the dimly lit streets of Bermondsey. In Whitechapel, her father would have been making his rounds by now, bringing light to the darkness. Here, the lamps seemed fewer, the shadows deeper.

"No one even looked at me," she whispered, remembering

how everyone had chatted animatedly throughout dinner while she stood silently in the corner, waiting to clear their plates. "It's as if I'm not even here."

A tear slipped down her cheek, but she brushed it away roughly with the back of her hand. Her father's voice seemed to whisper in her ear: "Grace, my love, remember what I taught you. In this world, there will always be darkness, but we must be the ones to bring the light."

William had always stressed the importance of compassion, even when it wasn't returned. "Kindness isn't something you give because you expect it back," he'd told her once. "You give it because that's who you are."

Grace pulled her journal from beneath the mattress, along with a stub of pencil she'd managed to keep. By the faint moonlight, she began to write:

The Hartwells are not my family, though we share a name. Cornelius speaks little and looks through me. Agatha sees only what I haven't done, never what I have. Violet preens like a peacock with her fine things, and Humphrey delights in causing pain. Yet Father would say to look deeper. Perhaps they too have sorrows I cannot see.

Writing calmed her, ordering her thoughts and giving shape to her fears. When she finished, Grace tucked the journal away and lay down on the thin mattress, pulling the threadbare blanket over her shoulders. She clutched her mother's prayer book and locket to her chest, the metal warm against her skin.

Sleep refused to come. The unfamiliar creaks of the house, the distant sounds of carriages on the street, the weight of uncertainty pressing down—all conspired to keep her awake. What would tomorrow bring? More work, certainly. More coldness. More feeling like a ghost in a house full of the living.

"I don't know if I can bear it," she whispered into the darkness.

As if in answer, Grace's mind conjured her mother's face—not from memory, for she had none, but from the stories her father had told and the tiny portrait in the locket. Her mother's gentle eyes seemed to gaze at her with understanding.

"Help comes when it is needed most," she imagined her mother saying. "And sometimes, my darling, you must be the help that others need, even when they don't know it."

The thought brought an unexpected peace. Grace's eyelids grew heavy, and as sleep finally claimed her, she made a silent promise: she would find a way to share her mother's healing spirit in this house. Even in the coldness of the Hartwell home, she would kindle a flame of warmth—just as her father had brought light to London's darkest streets.

8

CHORES

The cock had not yet crowed when Grace's eyes fluttered open in the dim attic. Dawn barely whispered through the small window as she peeled herself from the straw mattress, its scratchy surface having left red marks along her arms. Her breath clouded before her face in the frigid morning air.

Grace shivered, pulling her thin dress over her nightgown for added warmth. No time to change properly—Agatha expected the fire lit before the family stirred. She tucked her mother's locket beneath her collar, the cool metal warming against her skin, a small comfort as she faced another day in this cold house.

The stairs protested beneath her careful steps. Third from the top creaked loudest—she'd learned to skip it entirely, placing one foot on the fourth stair and stretching to reach the second. The banister felt rough beneath her palm, splinters threatening her tender skin.

In the kitchen hearth, last night's embers had died to grey ash. Grace knelt before it, her knees pressing against the hard stone floor. She brushed away yesterday's remnants, the fine powder coating her fingers and floating upward to tickle her nose. She stifled a sneeze—noise would wake the house before its time.

"Father always said a good fire starts with patience," she whispered to herself, arranging kindling in a careful pyramid.

The smell of smoke rose as the first flames caught, carrying her thoughts back to mornings in their rooms above the bakery. Her father stoking the small stove, his voice gentle as he recited morning prayers. The memory warmed her more than the growing fire before her.

Grace had just begun to fill the copper kettle when footsteps sounded on the stairs. Heavy, deliberate steps—Agatha. She straightened her back, tucking loose strands of hair behind her ears.

"The floors need scrubbing before breakfast," Agatha announced, her eyes narrowing as she surveyed the kitchen. "The children have their lessons today, and I won't have them walking on filth."

"Yes, Mrs Hartwell," Grace replied, reaching for the wooden bucket.

On her knees, Grace worked the scrub brush in wide arcs across the floorboards. The soap stung the cracks in her chapped hands, but she dared not slow her pace. Agatha stood by the doorway, arms folded across her chest, watching each movement with the intensity of a predator.

"You've missed a spot there," Agatha's voice cut through the silence. "And there. Are your eyes not working, girl? Or is it your mind that's lacking?"

Grace bit her lip, scrubbing harder at the indicated spots. The wood beneath her brush was already clean, but she knew better than to argue.

"The corners, girl! How many times must I tell you about the corners?"

Grace shuffled backward on her knees, moving to clean the joint between floor and wall. The brush slipped from her wet fingers, clattering against the floorboards.

Agatha's patience snapped. She stormed across the wet floor, her skirts swishing angrily. "Clumsy girl!" Her foot caught the bucket, sending dirty water cascading across Grace's freshly scrubbed floor.

"Look what you've done now!" Agatha's hand came down hard across Grace's back. The sudden blow knocked the air from her lungs, leaving a stinging pain that blossomed between her shoulder blades.

"I'm sorry, Mrs Hartwell," Grace gasped, fighting back tears that threatened to spill.

"Clean it up. And be quick about it—the children will want their breakfast."

Grace sopped up the spilled water, her back throbbing with each movement. By the time she'd finished, her dress clung damp and cold against her skin. She hurried to prepare porridge, stirring the oats into boiling water as Violet and Humphrey's voices echoed down the stairwell.

"Is breakfast ready yet?" Humphrey demanded, sliding into his chair at the table. "I'm starving!"

Grace placed a steaming bowl before him, careful not to spill a drop. "Yes, Master Humphrey. Just as you like it."

His nose wrinkled as he poked at the porridge with his spoon. "It's lumpy. I hate lumpy porridge."

"Mine isn't sweet enough," Violet complained, pushing her bowl away. "Did you even add any sugar at all?"

Grace's stomach twisted with hunger as she watched them toy with food she would have gratefully eaten. "I'll add more sugar to yours, Miss Violet," she offered, reaching for the small bowl of precious sugar.

"Don't waste good sugar on her complaints," Agatha snapped from the doorway. "Violet, eat what you're given. The girl has other chores to attend to."

Grace stood with her hands folded, face carefully blank as the children continued their breakfast, occasionally shooting her dirty looks between reluctant spoonfuls. Inside, her heart ached for the loving mornings she'd once known, but her face revealed nothing of the storm within.

9
SMALL KINDNESS

The afternoon sun slanted through the small, grimy window of the attic, casting long shadows across the rough wooden floor. Grace had finished scrubbing the entryway tiles and polishing the brass doorknobs to Agatha's exacting standards. The Hartwells had gone to visit acquaintances, leaving Grace alone with a list of chores longer than her arm.

She listened carefully for any sounds from below. Silence. Blessed silence.

Grace pulled her mother's prayer book from beneath her thin mattress, the leather binding worn smooth by years of faithful hands. She crept to the far corner of the attic where a small nook formed between a discarded trunk and the sloping roof. Kneeling on the hard floor, she opened the book to a familiar page, tracing the faded ink with her fingertip.

"The Lord is my shepherd; I shall not want," she whispered, the words flowing from memory rather than sight. "He maketh me to lie down in green pastures: he leadeth me beside the still waters."

The attic dust danced in the shaft of sunlight as Grace's whispered prayers filled the small space. Each verse connected her to her father—to evenings spent by candlelight as he taught her the words that had sustained her mother through difficult times.

"Though I walk through the valley of the shadow of death, I will fear no evil: for thou art with me."

Tears pricked at her eyes, but Grace blinked them away. These moments were too precious for weeping. The prayer book's pages held more than Scripture; they contained her mother's gentle touch, her father's steady voice, a reminder that she had once been loved completely.

"Surely goodness and mercy shall follow me all the days of my life."

Grace closed the book and pressed it to her chest, feeling her heartbeat against the worn leather. These stolen moments of prayer were bridges spanning the chasm between her past and present, reminding her that somewhere beyond the Hartwells' cold walls, goodness still existed.

A church bell tolled in the distance. Grace tucked the prayer book away and hurried downstairs. Agatha had instructed her to fetch bread from the baker before they returned. This errand, though meant as a chore, felt like freedom.

Outside, the narrow streets bustled with afternoon activity. Grace clutched the few pennies Agatha had grudgingly provided, making her way toward the bakery. At the corner of Bell Lane, a familiar mewling caught her attention.

"Hello there," she whispered, kneeling beside an over-turned crate where three cats huddled together—a tabby with a torn ear, a black cat with white paws, and a skinny ginger kitten.

From her pocket, Grace pulled a small bundle wrapped in paper—crusts from the Hartwells' breakfast that she'd saved rather than thrown away. The cats approached cautiously, their whiskers twitching at the scent of food.

"Careful now," she murmured, breaking the bread into smaller pieces. "There's enough for all."

The tabby rubbed against her skirt, purring loudly enough that Grace felt the vibration through the thin fabric. The black cat kept its distance but watched with intelligent eyes as it accepted a morsel from her outstretched palm. The ginger kitten, bolder than its companions, climbed onto her lap, its tiny body warm against her cold hands.

"You're getting braver, aren't you?" Grace stroked its head, feeling the tension in her shoulders ease as the kitten purred. "I've named you Ember, for your colour. Like the embers in the hearth that keep the house warm."

For a precious few minutes, Grace forgot about the Hartwells and their endless demands. Here, among London's forgotten creatures, she found unexpected kinship. These cats asked nothing of her but the scraps she could spare, offering affection without judgment.

Other strays emerged from shadowy corners—a one-eyed tom she called Captain, a sleek grey she'd named Shadow. They recognised her now, these street cats of Bermondsey, gathering whenever she appeared with her small offerings.

"I must go," she said reluctantly, gently setting Ember back beside its companions. "But I'll return tomorrow if I can."

As Grace continued toward the bakery, her step was lighter, her back straighter. The cats' simple gratitude had kindled something within her—a reminder that even in this harsh world, she could still bring comfort to others. In those brief encounters, she wasn't the unwanted orphan or the household drudge, but Grace Hartwell, daughter of William and Mary, capable of kindness in a world that had shown her precious little.

10

PRIVATE VICTORIES

The Hartwell household settled into its evening routine, with Cornelius retreating to his study and Agatha busying herself with needlework in the parlour. Grace moved quietly through the kitchen, cleaning the last of the dinner dishes when a small figure appeared in the doorway.

Violet stood there, her usual haughty demeanour diminished by flushed cheeks and watery eyes. Her golden curls hung limp around her face, and she clutched her doll tightly against her chest.

"I don't feel well," she whimpered, her voice raspy and thin.

Grace set down the plate she'd been drying and approached the girl cautiously. "What hurts, Violet?"

"My throat feels like fire," Violet said, uncharacteristically vulnerable. "And my head aches something terrible."

Grace placed her palm against Violet's forehead. The skin burned beneath her touch. Without thinking, she guided the child to a chair.

"Stay here," Grace instructed gently. "I'll fetch your mother."

Agatha's reaction was predictable. "A cold? Children get colds. She'll be fine by morning." She barely looked up from her embroidery. "Just put her to bed."

"She has a fever, Mrs Hartwell," Grace persisted. "Perhaps some willow bark tea might—"

"Nonsense," Agatha snapped. "We don't believe in those country remedies. Just see that she drinks water and goes to sleep."

Grace bit her tongue and nodded, returning to the kitchen where Violet sat slumped in the chair, her doll dangling precariously from her fingertips.

As she helped Violet upstairs, Grace's mind raced through memories of her father's teachings. Her mother had known remedies for nearly every ailment, knowledge William had passed on to Grace in fragments and stories.

"My throat hurts," Violet complained again as Grace tucked her into bed.

"I know," Grace whispered. "Rest now. I'll bring you something to help."

Once Violet had settled, Grace slipped down to the kitchen. She glanced about, ensuring she was alone before opening the small pantry. Behind jars of preserves, she found what she needed—a small pot of honey and dried basil leaves that Agatha kept for cooking.

Working quickly, Grace boiled water and steeped the basil, adding a generous spoonful of honey once the mixture had cooled slightly. The sweet, aromatic scent reminded her of evenings with her father, of his gentle hands guiding hers as they prepared similar concoctions for neighbours with winter ailments.

"This will soothe your throat," Grace explained as she helped Violet sit up in bed. "Small sips, now."

Violet wrinkled her nose at the strange brew but obeyed, too miserable to protest. After several tentative sips, her tense shoulders relaxed slightly.

"It tastes strange," she murmured, "but nice."

"My mother used to make it," Grace said softly. "My father said she could heal anyone with her remedies."

Violet's eyes widened slightly. "Was she a witch?"

Grace smiled, the first genuine smile she'd shared with any of the Hartwells. "No. Just a faith-filled woman who understood plants and their secrets."

She continued administering the remedy throughout the evening, slipping into Violet's room between chores. By morning, the girl's fever had broken, and though still weak, her eyes were clearer, her breathing easier.

"The child looks better," Mrs Finley, the neighbour who often visited Agatha for tea, observed the next afternoon. "I heard her coughing yesterday. Sounded dreadful."

"Grace made me a special drink," Violet announced before her mother could respond. "With honey and herbs. It tasted funny but made my throat stop hurting."

Agatha's lips thinned to a tight line. "Nonsense. It was simply a good night's rest."

But Mrs Finley's gaze lingered on Grace, who kept her eyes lowered as she served the tea. "Is that so? My Tommy's been plagued with a similar ailment. Perhaps ..."

"Grace has chores to attend to," Agatha interrupted sharply. "Don't you, girl?"

Grace nodded and retreated to the kitchen, but not before catching Mrs Finley's thoughtful expression.

Later that night, in the solitude of her attic room, Grace pulled out her journal by the dim light of a candle stub. The pages were already filling with her careful notes—drawings of plants, recipes for tinctures and poultices, memories of her father's stories about her mother's healing work.

Today I helped Violet, she wrote. *The basil and honey worked just as Father said it would. I felt Mother's presence as I prepared it, as though her hands guided mine.*

Grace paused, listening to the quiet house below. Through the thin floor, she could hear Violet's improved breathing, no longer laboured with congestion.

I wonder if this is what Mother felt—this warmth that comes from easing another's suffering. Even Violet's, who has shown me little kindness.

Her pencil moved across the page, recording dreams too precious to speak aloud.

Someday, perhaps, I might help others beyond these walls. A proper healer, with knowledge of herbs and remedies. Not just the orphan girl or the household drudge, but someone who brings light to dark places, as Father did with his lamps and Mother with her healing touch.

The weeks turned to months, and though Agatha's treatment remained harsh, Grace found small ways to nurture her growing knowledge. She created a tiny garden of medicinal herbs in a forgotten corner behind the coal shed, tending it during rare moments of freedom.

Each morning, Grace rose before dawn, no longer dreading Agatha's sharp commands but meeting them with quiet resolve. The cruelty that once threatened to crush her spirit now fuelled a determination that burned steadily within her chest.

"You'll never amount to anything," Agatha often muttered when Grace's work failed to meet her impossible standards.

Grace would lower her eyes, hiding the fire that flickered

behind them. *You're wrong,* she thought. *I am my mother's daughter, my father's child. Their light lives in me.*

In her secret garden, Grace cultivated more than plants. She nurtured hope, knowledge, and plans for a future beyond the Hartwells' narrow walls. Each leaf she tended, each remedy she committed to memory was a silent rebellion against the limitations others sought to place upon her.

And sometimes, when neighbours whispered of ailments, Grace found ways to leave small bundles of herbs on doorsteps or offer quiet suggestions that were increasingly heeded. These small acts of healing became her private victory, a reminder that even in the darkest circumstances, she could still bring light.

11

A BREWING STORM

Grace dried the last plate and returned it to the cupboard, satisfied with the gleaming surfaces she'd created despite her aching back. She'd spent the day scrubbing floors, mending linens, and preparing supper—tasks that had become second nature after nearly five years in the Hartwell household. The evening quiet was a rare blessing, with Violet and Humphrey already settled in the parlour with their games, and Agatha occupied with her needlework.

The distant sound of uneven footsteps on the front steps shattered the tranquility. Grace stiffened, recognising the heavy, stumbling gait of Cornelius returning home. The clock on the mantel showed half past nine—hours later than his usual arrival.

Agatha's head snapped up from her embroidery, her needle poised mid-stitch. Her mouth tightened into a thin line as she set her work aside and moved toward the entryway. Grace retreated deeper into the kitchen shadows, watching through the crack in the door.

"Children, continue with your game," Agatha instructed, her voice brittle with forced calm.

The front door swung open with unnecessary force, banging against the wall. Cornelius lurched inside, his coat askew and hat tilted at an odd angle. The sour smell of gin and tobacco seeped into the house, causing Grace to wrinkle her nose.

"Evening, family," he slurred, attempting a smile that looked more like a grimace.

Violet and Humphrey exchanged worried glances, their usual boisterous chatter silenced. Humphrey's wooden soldiers remained frozen on the carpet, the battle forgotten as a different kind of tension filled the room.

"Where have you been?" Agatha hissed, low enough that she thought the children couldn't hear, but Grace caught every word from her vantage point. "And in this state?"

Cornelius waved a dismissive hand, nearly losing his balance in the process. "Business matters. Nothing for you to worry about."

"Father?" Violet ventured, her voice small. "Would you like to see the drawing I made today?"

Cornelius blinked at his daughter as if just noticing her presence. "Later, girl. Later."

Grace's stomach knotted as she observed Violet's face fall. Despite everything, she felt a pang of sympathy for the child. The tension in the room was as thick as London fog, and Grace knew from experience that such storms rarely passed without breaking.

DAWN CREPT RELUCTANTLY through the attic window as Grace dressed in the half-light. She'd slept poorly, the raised voices from below having continued long after she'd retreated to her room. Now the house felt unnaturally quiet, tense with unspoken words.

She padded down the narrow stairs, careful to avoid the creaky third step. The kitchen was cold—no fire had been lit yet. Unusual. Typically, Agatha would be barking orders by now, criticising Grace's every movement as she prepared breakfast.

Grace knelt at the grate, arranging kindling just as her father had taught her. The familiar routine brought a fleeting comfort that vanished when she caught the sound of hushed, urgent voices from the parlour.

"What do you mean, dismissed?" Agatha's voice, though lowered, carried an edge sharper than any knife in the kitchen.

"Keep your voice down," Cornelius hissed. "The children—"

"The children will know soon enough when there's no food on the table!"

Grace's hands froze mid-task. Dismissed? Her stomach clenched as the implications crystallised in her mind.

"Mr Pemberton gave me chances. Three warnings about the drinking." Cornelius's voice cracked. "Said I was unreliable. That my ledgers had errors."

"And what are we to do now? How are we to live?" The panic in Agatha's tone sent a chill through Grace's bones.

"I'll find something else. I have connections—"

"Connections? The same connections that keep you in gin until all hours?"

Grace struck the flint harder than necessary, sparks flying as the kindling caught. The fire reflected the burning anxiety in her chest. Without Cornelius's position, what little security she had would surely vanish. They barely tolerated her presence when they could afford to feed her.

She moved to the pantry, counting the remaining potatoes and the half-sack of flour. Not enough. Not nearly enough.

The parlour door slammed open. Grace jumped, nearly dropping the flour scoop.

"You!" Agatha stood in the doorway, her face blotched with anger. "What are you doing?"

"Preparing breakfast, ma'am," Grace answered, keeping her voice steady.

"Did you hear?" Agatha's eyes narrowed suspiciously.

"No, ma'am."

"Liar." The word hung between them like poison. "Well, you might as well know. Cornelius here has lost his position. Lost it through his own foolishness and vice."

Grace lowered her eyes, saying nothing.

"Do you understand what this means, girl?" Agatha stepped closer. "We can barely feed our own children now."

The threat remained unspoken but clear as crystal. Grace felt her place in this household, already precarious, slipping away entirely.

"I don't require much, ma'am," she ventured. "And I can work harder—"

"Work?" Agatha laughed, a brittle sound devoid of humour. "And who will pay for this work? We have mouths to feed. Real family."

Grace retreated to her small room during a brief respite from chores, her hands trembling as she reached for her mother's prayer book hidden beneath her thin mattress. The leather was worn smooth from years of desperate touches, the pages fragile with age and use.

She clutched it to her chest, fingers tracing the faded gold cross on its cover. Downstairs, the argument had resumed, voices rising and falling like a violent tide. Through the floorboards came Agatha's shrill accusations and Cornelius's slurred defences.

Grace sat on her bed, prayer book pressed against her heart as though it could shield her from what was coming. This small treasure, along with her mother's locket and her father's badge, were all that remained of a life where she'd been loved. The thought of losing her place, however miserable, filled her with cold dread.

"Not my book," she whispered, holding it tighter. "Whatever happens, they shan't take this from me."

12

THE FOLLOWING DAYS

The following days in the Hartwell household unfolded like a bitter winter—harsh, unrelenting, and without promise of spring. Grace rose earlier each morning, working her fingers raw before the family stirred, desperate to prove her worth through silent industry.

Agatha stalked the narrow corridors like a vengeful spirit, her face perpetually pinched with worry and resentment. Her eyes followed Grace's every movement, searching for flaws to expose, for mistakes to punish.

"Look at this dust!" Agatha rubbed a finger across the mantelpiece Tuesday morning, though Grace had polished it not an hour before. "Useless girl. Your father's position might have been humble, but at least he earned his keep."

Grace bowed her head, biting back words that would only invite further wrath. The mention of her father—a good man who'd brought light to dark streets—twisted in her chest like a knife.

"I'm sorry, ma'am. I'll do it again."

"Sorry doesn't fill empty bellies, does it?" Agatha's voice rose, carrying through the house. "We've mouths to feed—proper family mouths—not charity cases picked up out of pity!"

In the parlour, Violet and Humphrey froze in their play, eyes wide as their mother's tirade continued. Cornelius had taken to spending his days away from home, returning only to sleep, leaving Agatha's frustrations to boil over unchecked.

"Do you know what it costs to feed an extra mouth? To clothe it? To heat the very air it breathes?" Agatha jabbed a finger toward Grace. "And what do we get in return? Half-done chores and sullen looks."

Grace scrubbed harder at the floor, her knees aching against the wooden boards. The lye soap burned her cracked hands, but she welcomed the sting—it gave her something to focus on besides the cruel words raining down.

"Perhaps Mrs Finley needs a scullery maid," Agatha mused aloud later that afternoon, measuring flour with sharp, angry movements. "Though I doubt she'd take you. Too skinny for proper work. Too dreamy-headed."

Grace stood silently by the sink, washing dishes with mechanical precision. Her mother's locket pressed against her thigh through the fabric of her pocket—a small, secret weight that anchored her to who she truly was. Not this "burden," this "charity case," but the daughter of William and Mary Hartwell.

"Or the workhouse might take you," Agatha continued, her voice casual as though discussing the weather rather than Grace's fate. "Though they say conditions there are quite dreadful. Not that you're accustomed to luxury here."

The word "workhouse" sent a chill through Grace's bones. She'd heard whispers of such places—families torn apart, children worked until they dropped, disease running rampant through crowded dormitories. She scrubbed a pot with renewed vigour, as if she could scour away the threat.

Thursday brought rain that hammered against the windows, matching Agatha's mood. Grace had been sent to market with too little money and instructions to bargain fiercely. When she returned with slightly bruised vegetables—all she could afford—Agatha's face contorted with disgust.

"This is what you bring back? Even in our reduced circumstances, we're not animals to eat such slop!"

"The good produce was twice the price, ma'am," Grace explained quietly. "I thought—"

"You thought?" Agatha laughed, the sound brittle as thin ice. "That's the trouble with you, isn't it? Always thinking you know better, with your herbs and your remedies and your airs."

She snatched the basket, examining each item with exaggerated revulsion. "A burden. That's what you are. A burden we can no longer afford."

The words struck Grace like physical blows. She stood perfectly still, feeling the weight of her mother's locket against her leg. Within its small circle of silver lay her mother's portrait—a woman who had loved her, who had passed down knowledge of healing rather than hurting.

That night, as Grace knelt to scrub the kitchen floor after dinner, Agatha stood over her, arms crossed.

"You'll need to work twice as hard now," she said, her voice cold. "Every morsel you eat must be earned. Every thread on your back. Every breath you take in this house."

Grace nodded, keeping her eyes on the dark floorboards beneath her brush. Her knees ached, her back throbbed, but her hands moved steadily, rhythmically across the wood.

"Yes, ma'am," she murmured.

As Agatha finally left, Grace slipped her hand into her

pocket, fingers closing around the locket. The metal had warmed against her skin, as if holding some small flame within—a reminder that once, she had been cherished. That once, she had been enough.

And perhaps, someday, she would be again.

13
FORCED FREEDOM

Another week passed with tension thick as Thames fog in the Hartwell household. Grace moved through her chores like a ghost, keeping her head down and her voice soft, hoping to avoid Agatha's wrath. Cornelius remained absent most days, returning late with empty pockets and the sour stench of cheap gin.

That Friday afternoon, Grace was scrubbing the kitchen floor when the front door crashed open. Cornelius stumbled in, his collar askew, face flushed not from drink but from something worse—humiliation. He stood in the doorway, rainwater dripping from his coat onto the floor Grace had just cleaned.

"Another rejection," he muttered, more to himself than to Grace. "Not even the shipping office would have me. Said my references were poor."

Grace kept her eyes on the floorboards, scrubbing harder. If she remained invisible, perhaps his dark mood would pass over her.

Agatha appeared from the parlour, her face tightening at the sight of her husband. "Nothing again, then?"

Cornelius threw his sodden hat onto the side table. "What do you think? Would I look like this if I'd found work?"

His gaze fell on Grace, kneeling with her brush and bucket. Something shifted in his expression—the shame transforming into something harder, meaner.

"Look at her," he said, jabbing a finger toward Grace. "On her knees like she's doing us some great service. While we struggle to keep a roof over our heads."

Grace's hands stilled. She'd learned to weather Agatha's storms, but Cornelius rarely directed his bitterness toward her so directly.

"I've done my best to earn my keep, sir," she said quietly.

"Your keep?" Cornelius barked a laugh. "Do you have any idea what it costs to feed and house you? And for what? So you can play at being a servant?"

Agatha moved beside her husband, emboldened by his rage. "We've clothed you, fed you, given you shelter when no one else would. And what have we got in return? A sullen, ungrateful girl who thinks she's above her station."

"I never—" Grace began, but Cornelius cut her off.

"You've been nothing but a drain on this family from the moment you arrived," he spat. "A worthless street girl we took in out of charity."

Grace felt the ground beneath her knees shift, a terrible understanding dawning. This wasn't just another tirade. Something had changed.

Cornelius continued, his voice rising, "We can barely feed our own children. Why should we continue supporting you?"

Agatha's eyes glinted. "She's seventeen now. Old enough to make her own way."

Seventeen. The word hung in the air between them. Old enough that they no longer felt obligated to shelter her, young enough that the world outside would show her no mercy.

"I can work harder," Grace said, rising to her feet, the brush still clutched in her hand. "I can find employment elsewhere and contribute—"

"It's too late for that," Cornelius said. He strode past her, taking the stairs two at a time.

Grace stood frozen as his heavy footsteps moved above, followed by the sound of her attic door being flung open. When he returned, he carried her small bundle of possessions —two worn dresses, a patched shawl, her fathers' badge, and her mother's prayer book.

"This is all you came with," he said, thrusting the items toward her. "And this is all you'll leave with."

Grace's heart hammered against her ribs. "Please, Mr Hartwell. My family—"

"We are not your family." He snarled, moving toward the door and flinging it open. The cold afternoon air rushed in, carrying the scent of more rain coming.

With a violent motion, he threw her belongings onto the wet street. The prayer book landed in a puddle, its pages instantly darkening with water.

"No!" Grace lunged forward, but Agatha grabbed her arm.

"Where do you think you're going, girl?" Her fingers dug into Grace's flesh. "That locket around your neck—it's far too fine for someone like you."

Grace's hand flew to her throat, where her mother's locket hung on its thin chain. "It was my mother's—"

"And now it will pay for some of what you've cost us," Agatha said, reaching for the chain.

Grace twisted away, panic surging through her. "No! You can't have it!"

Agatha's nails scratched Grace's neck as she clawed at the locket. "Ungrateful wretch! After all we've done for you!"

Something broke inside Grace—years of quiet submission shattered by this final cruelty. She wrenched herself free with surprising strength, clutching the locket in her fist.

"This is all I have left of my mother!" she cried, her voice ringing with a ferocity that seemed to surprise even herself. "This and her prayer book are the only pieces of my family I have left in this world. They hold her spirit—her memory. I will not let you take them from me!"

Agatha recoiled, momentarily stunned by Grace's outburst. In that instant of hesitation, Grace darted past her, out the door and into the street. She fell to her knees, gathering her soaked belongings, cradling the waterlogged prayer book against her chest.

"Don't come back," Cornelius called after her. "You're no longer welcome in this house."

Grace struggled to her feet, clutching her meagre possessions. The locket hung heavy around her neck, her mother's face pressed against her skin beneath her dress. The prayer book dripped water down her arms.

The door slammed behind her with terrible finality. Five years of her life sealed away behind that wooden barrier.

She stood alone on the stret, the reality of her situation crashing over her like the first drops of rain that began to fall. Bermondsey's narrow streets stretched before her, shadows lengthening as afternoon faded toward evening. The world suddenly seemed vast and hostile, full of unknown dangers.

But the locket remained around her neck, and the prayer book, though damaged, was still in her possession. She had protected what mattered most—the last connections to her true family, to people who had loved her completely.

Drawing a deep breath, Grace stepped away from the Hartwell house, her back straightening despite the weight of uncertainty pressing down upon her. She had nothing but the clothes on her back, a few damp garments, and her treasured mementos. Yet somehow, as she walked away from the cold house that had never truly been a home, she felt the first stirring of something unexpected.

Freedom.

14
LIGHT

Grace moved through the crowded streets of Bermondsey, her damp belongings clutched to her chest. The world had transformed in the span of minutes—familiar corners now loomed threatening, once-friendly store-fronts seemed to glare with suspicion. People bustled past, their shoulders occasionally knocking against hers, their faces blank and uninterested in the plight of yet another homeless girl.

The smells of the neighbourhood—coal smoke, rotting vegetables from the market, the occasional waft of bread from a bakery—struck her with painful clarity. That bakery scent twisted in her chest, conjuring memories of Mr Grigson's shop, of sitting by the warm oven with her father as he told stories of her mother. William's steady voice, the feel of his rough hand on her shoulder, the crinkle around his eyes when he smiled—all of it gone, replaced by the indifferent tide of London's masses.

A woman with a basket of washing stepped around Grace as though she were a lamppost or rubbish bin—just another obstacle in the street. A pair of boys kicked a ball dangerously close to her feet without a glance in her direction. Their laughter stung her ears.

"Pardon, miss," muttered a cart driver, not waiting for her response as his wheels splashed through a puddle, speckling her already sodden skirts with muddy water.

Grace clutched her mother's prayer book tighter, its pages still dripping. The ink had begun to blur, her mother's careful notations in the margins dissolving into watery smudges. The sight of it sent a fresh wave of panic through her.

She hurried to a narrow alley between buildings, crouching to spread the book open, pages fanned across her lap. Trembling fingers smoothed the delicate paper, willing the words to remain. Some pages had stuck together, others threatened to tear with the gentlest touch.

"Please," she whispered, though she wasn't certain who she addressed—God, her mother, or the book itself. "Please don't fade away."

When the pages had dried enough to handle, Grace carefully closed the book and tucked it beneath her shawl. She emerged from the alley, surveying the streets with new eyes— the eyes of someone without shelter or protection.

Whitechapel lay to the east, where she had spent her earliest years with her father. Perhaps someone there might remember William Hartwell's daughter. But five years had passed, and London's memory was short when it came to the poor. The journey would take hours on foot, and night approached.

St Mary Magdalen church stood a few streets away. The vicar might offer shelter, at least for tonight. But she'd heard whispers of girls sent to workhouses by well-meaning clergy who believed it the proper place for orphans.

Grace wandered into a small square where a patch of

scraggly grass and three benches constituted what passed for a park in this part of London. She sank onto a bench, her legs suddenly too weak to carry her further. The weight of her situation crashed over her like a wave.

Tears welled and spilled down her cheeks. She made no sound as they fell, having learned long ago in the Hartwell household that silent crying drew less attention. Her fingers found the locket at her throat, tracing its oval shape, the tiny engraving around its edge.

"Mother," she whispered, opening the locket to reveal Mary's face, painted in delicate strokes. The portrait showed a woman with Grace's same fiery red hair and gentle eyes. "I'm alone now. Truly alone."

The painted face offered no response, yet Grace felt something stir within her—a warmth that began in her chest and spread outward. She remembered her father's stories of Mary Hartwell, who had tended the sick and poor without hesitation, who had sung hymns while brewing her remedies, who had loved fiercely and completely.

"You would have known what to do," Grace murmured, wiping her tears with the back of her hand. "You would have found a way forward."

A memory surfaced—her father's voice, steady and sure: "Your mother believed that even in our darkest moments, we carry light within us. That's why she helped others, Grace. She believed in sharing that light."

Grace closed the locket, feeling its weight against her skin. She looked down at her mother's prayer book, damaged but not destroyed. Within those pages lay not just prayers, but recipes for healing, notes on which herbs soothed fevers and eased pain, wisdom passed from mother to daughter.

"I will carry your light," she promised, her voice steadying. "I will help others as you would have done."

The sun began its descent, casting long shadows across the small park and painting the clouds in brilliant orange. Grace rose from the bench, gathering her few possessions. She had no destination, no plan beyond surviving the night, yet something had shifted within her. The terror remained, but alongside it grew a fragile determination.

She walked with purpose now, scanning doorways and sheltered corners. Near the docks, she found a recessed doorway to a shuttered shop, deep enough to offer some protection from the elements. Grace settled there as darkness fell, arranging her shawl as both blanket and curtain.

"Guide me through this night," she whispered, one hand on her locket, the other on her prayer book. "Help me find my way."

As the city's lamps flickered to life—lit by men like her father had once been—Grace closed her eyes, prepared to face whatever tomorrow might bring.

15
ON THE STREETS

The first grey fingers of dawn stretched across the skyline as Grace uncurled from her makeshift shelter. Her limbs ached from the hard ground, and the morning chill had settled deep into her bones. She shook out her skirt, smoothed her hair as best she could without a brush, and ventured into the awakening city.

The city transformed at dawn. Carts rattled over cobblestones, merchants shouted orders, and dock workers trudged to their posts. Grace observed this dance of commerce with new eyes—not as a passing observer, but as someone who must now find her place within it.

Near Bermondsey Market, children scurried between stalls, selling everything from matches to yesterday's newspapers. A girl no older than ten held out bunches of wilting violets to passing ladies, her voice high and pleading. A boy darted through the crowd with bootlaces draped over his arm, calling out prices in a practised singsong.

Grace approached the violet girl cautiously. "Where do you get your flowers?"

The girl eyed her suspiciously. "Why? You looking to take my patch?"

"No, I just—I need to earn something. Anything."

The girl's face softened slightly. "Covent Garden. Early morning. Get the castoffs from the big sellers." She glanced at Grace's relatively clean dress. "Though you won't last long in that. Might try matches first. Easier to carry."

By midday, Grace had acquired a small box of matches from a sympathetic vendor who'd taken pity on her story. She positioned herself on a corner near a tea shop, holding out her wares with trembling hands.

"Matches, sir? Only a ha'penny for three."

Her first attempts were met with indifference. People brushed past without a glance, or worse, with looks of disdain. Grace observed the other children—how they called out with cheerful persistence, how they positioned themselves where foot traffic slowed naturally, how they targeted certain types of passers-by.

A woman with a kind face approached, and Grace smiled tentatively. "Matches, ma'am? Finest quality."

The woman paused. "You're new to this, aren't you, dear?"

Grace hesitated, then nodded.

"Stand where the wind won't catch your voice. And smile more—you've a lovely smile." The woman purchased six matches, paying a full penny. "God bless you, child."

Grace was grateful she looked younger than her seventeen years. People seemed to be kinder to the younger children.

That penny bought Grace a small loaf of bread—her first meal in nearly twenty-four hours. She savoured each bite, making it last as she continued her efforts through the afternoon.

Days melted into weeks as autumn deepened into winter. Grace learned to navigate the unspoken territories of street vendors, to spot which policemen turned a blind eye and which would chase children away with threats of the work-house. She discovered that certain corners yielded better results, that smiling genuinely despite her circumstances drew more customers than desperate pleas.

16

A NEW FAMILY

Gradually, Grace found herself moving across the city of London. She did her best to avoid both Bermondsey and Whitechapel, as the memories linked to both places still stung too much. When the first frost settled over London, Grace faced the bitter reality of winter on the streets. Her thin shawl offered little protection against the biting wind. Her boots, already worn when she'd left the Hartwells, now sported holes that let in every puddle of freezing rain.

One particularly brutal evening, as sleet pelted the streets, Grace huddled beneath London Bridge, pressed against the stone wall. Her day's earnings—three farthings—weren't enough for a night's lodging. She wrapped her arms around her knees, shivering violently as hunger gnawed at her stomach.

"Please," she whispered, touching her locket. "Help me find strength."

A shadow fell across her, and Grace looked up, tensing. A boy of perhaps fifteen stood there, his face smudged with grime, clothes more ragged than her own.

"You're in my spot," he said, but without malice.

"I'm sorry. I'll move."

"Nah." He plopped down beside her. "Cold enough to share tonight. I'm Ronny."

"Grace."

Ronny produced a small, slightly squashed bun from his pocket. "Split it?"

Grace's pride warred with her hunger. "I couldn't—"

"Take it. Tomorrow you might have something I don't." He broke the bun, offering her the larger half. "That's how it works out here."

That night marked the beginning of Grace's street family. Through Ronny, she met others—Lizzie with her gap-toothed smile, Tom who could whistle like a songbird, Sarah who knew every shortcut in the East End. They shared what little they had, warned each other of dangers, and huddled together on the coldest nights.

Grace's knowledge of remedies became invaluable. When Lizzie developed a hacking cough, Grace gathered herbs from the edges of parks to brew a soothing tea. When Tom cut his foot on broken glass, she cleaned and bandaged it with strips torn from her petticoat.

"It's like magic," Ronny declared after Grace eased his earache with a poultice. "Angel Grace, that's what you are."

The name spread among the children. "Angel Grace knows what to do," they'd say when illness struck. The nickname warmed her even as winter tightened its grip on London.

One blustery morning while selling matches near the docks, Grace noticed an elderly woman struggling with buckets of flowers, her face twisted in pain as she tried to set up her stall.

"Let me help you," Grace offered, rushing forward to steady a toppling bucket.

The woman looked up, rheumy eyes assessing Grace. "Got strength in those arms, have you?"

"Enough," Grace replied, already arranging the flowers with care.

"I'm Maggie Bloom. Been selling posies here thirty years." She gestured to her leg. "Joints don't work like they used to."

Grace introduced herself, helping Maggie arrange her display. By noon, they'd sold half the flowers, with Grace's gentle manner drawing customers that might have passed by.

"You've a gift for this," Maggie observed. "And you need work, I can see that plain enough."

"I manage," Grace said, though her hollow cheeks told a different story.

"Listen here. You help me set up each morning, help sell through midday, I'll give you a corner of my pitch and teach you the trade." Maggie's weathered face crinkled into a smile. "Plus a hot tea each morning. Can't have those pretty hands turning blue, can we?"

For the first time since leaving the Hartwells, Grace felt a flicker of hope take root. "I'd be most grateful, Mrs Bloom."

"Maggie, girl. Just Maggie." She patted Grace's arm. "And between us, I know the best corners in all of London. Places where fine gentlemen pay extra for a bloom to give their ladies. I'll show you."

As they packed up the remaining flowers, Maggie shared stories of her decades on London's streets—of harsh winters survived, of kindnesses found in unexpected places, of the freedom that came with making one's own way despite the hardships.

"Life's taken much from you, I'd wager," Maggie said as they parted, "but it hasn't taken your spirit. That's what matters in the end."

Grace returned to Ronny and the others that evening with bread to share and news of her arrangement with Maggie. As they huddled together beneath their usual bridge, bellies slightly less empty than usual, Grace felt the stirring of something she'd almost forgotten—belonging.

17
A HEALING GIFT

January brought bitter winds and freezing fog. Grace awoke before dawn in the abandoned storehouse where she and the other children had found shelter, her breath forming clouds in the frigid air. Beside her, Ronny slept curled into a tight ball, his thin blanket barely covering his shoulders.

Grace tugged her shawl tighter and crept to the broken window. The streets below were silent, dusted with frost that glittered in the pale moonlight. Today would be another battle against the cold, but she had Maggie to think of now.

Old Maggie had fallen ill three days prior. What began as a slight wheeze had developed into a persistent, rattling cough that bent the elderly woman double. Yesterday, Grace had found her at the flower stall, face grey with exhaustion, handkerchief spotted with blood.

"It's nothing, love," Maggie had insisted. "Winter chest, that's all."

But Grace recognised the worry lining Maggie's weathered face. For a street vendor, illness meant no income, and no income meant no food, no shelter, no survival.

At the small hearth they'd fashioned from bricks, Grace kindled a tiny fire. From her pocket, she withdrew a cloth bundle containing dried thyme and the last precious spoonful of honey she'd traded three matches for. The herbs had been gathered from church gardens and park borders, each sprig carefully selected and dried over weeks.

"What're you brewing?" Ronny's sleepy voice came from behind her.

"Medicine for Maggie. Her cough's worsening."

Ronny sat beside her, watching as she steeped the herbs in the dented tin cup. "She's lucky to have you. We all are."

Grace smiled, remembering her father's words about her mother. "Mary could ease pain with just her touch," he'd told her. "It wasn't just the herbs—it was her care that healed people."

When the tea had steeped, Grace added the honey, stirring it with a sliver of wood. The sweet, herbal aroma filled their corner of the storehouse, drawing Lizzie and Tom from their slumber.

"Smells proper nice," Lizzie said, rubbing sleep from her eyes.

"Will there be any for us?" Tom asked hopefully.

Grace shook her head. "This is medicine for Maggie. But I'll make something for us tonight, I promise."

She poured a small portion into a chipped bottle she'd found, corking it carefully. The remainder she divided between her young friends, knowing they too needed strength against the cold.

By the time Grace reached Maggie's corner near the docks, the old woman was already attempting to arrange her meagre stock of winter blooms, pausing every few moments to double over with coughing.

"Here now," Grace said, rushing to steady her. "Sit down before you fall."

Maggie sank onto her wooden stool, wheezing. "Can't afford to rest, girl. These flowers won't sell themselves."

"They'll sell better if you're not frightening customers away with that cough." Grace produced her bottle. "Drink this. It's thyme and honey—my mother's remedy for winter chest."

Maggie eyed the bottle suspiciously. "Looks like muddy water."

"It works. Trust me."

The old woman took a sip, grimaced, then took another. "Not as foul as it looks," she admitted.

"Drink it all. I'll set up the stall."

As Grace arranged the flowers—snowdrops, winter jasmine, and early daffodils—she noticed Maggie's breathing ease slightly. By midday, the old woman's colour had improved, and she managed to charm several customers without coughing.

"Your medicine's done me good," Maggie said as they shared a crust of bread at noon. "Where'd you learn such things?"

"My mother was a healer. My father told me her remedies, and I've been collecting them in here." Grace tapped her journal. "Some I've figured out myself, watching what plants do."

Maggie studied her with newfound respect. "You've a gift, Angel Grace. A true gift."

Over the following weeks, Grace continued brewing remedies for Maggie while tending the flower stall. Word spread among the street vendors of the girl who could ease ailments with her herbal concoctions. Soon, mothers brought their coughing children, and elderly peddlers sought relief for their aching joints.

Grace never charged for her help, but people brought what

they could—a heel of bread, a worn but warm pair of gloves, occasionally even a copper or two. These small offerings she shared with Ronny and the others, their storehouse becoming a haven of sorts.

On Sundays, when the flower market closed early, they gathered in their shelter. Ronny would produce treasures scavenged throughout the week—a slightly dented tin of biscuits, apples past their prime but still sweet, once even a whole chicken pie liberated from a bakery's back step.

"To Angel Grace," Ronny toasted one evening, raising a cup of watered-down tea. "Who keeps us all breathing."

The others echoed his toast, their faces glowing in the firelight. Grace felt a warmth that had nothing to do with the small fire. This patchwork family, bound by necessity and survival, had become precious to her.

Each morning before dawn, Grace whispered prayers over her own cup of thyme tea, adding an extra pinch for strength. "Watch over Ronny," she murmured. "Keep Lizzie's cough at bay. Help Tom find good pickings today. Let Sarah stay warm."

Though frost painted the windows and hunger was never fully satisfied, Grace felt her parents' presence in these quiet moments. Her father's stories of bringing light to dark places. Her mother's legacy of healing hands. Both lived on through her, their love a flame that the bitter London winter couldn't extinguish.

18

A REFUGE

Grace trudged through the snow-laden streets, her thin shawl offering scant protection against the bitter evening wind. Maggie had closed the flower stall early—business slowed to nothing when the weather turned this foul. The few coins earned that day weighed in Grace's pocket, not enough for proper lodging but perhaps enough for a loaf to share with the others.

She turned down an unfamiliar alley, seeking shelter from the wind. The storehouse where they'd been sleeping had grown dangerously cold, with drafts whistling through broken windows. Ronny had mentioned looking for somewhere new, but they'd found nothing suitable yet.

As she rounded a corner, Grace stumbled against something hard and nearly fell. Steadying herself, she looked up at a weathered wooden sign swinging precariously from rusty chains. Most of the lettering had faded, but she could make out "...ley's Mercantile" in peeling paint.

Behind the sign stood a squat, abandoned building, its windows boarded but its door hanging partially open. Grace hesitated, then pushed the door wider. The hinges groaned in protest as she peered inside.

"Hello?" Her voice echoed in the emptiness.

No answer came. Grace slipped inside, relieved to escape the cutting wind. The interior was dusty but surprisingly intact—a forgotten place, bundled away from the elements. Weak moonlight filtered through cracks in the boarded windows, illuminating a large open space with a few smaller rooms branching off.

Grace explored cautiously. The main room must have been a shop once, with empty shelves lining the walls and a heavy counter at one end. Behind the counter, she discovered a small office with a pot-bellied stove, its chimney pipe still connected to a flue in the wall.

"Perfect," she whispered, running her hand along the stove's cold surface.

A decision formed in Grace's mind. This place could be more than temporary shelter—it could be a proper refuge for her makeshift family. Setting down her small bundle, she began to clear debris from around the stove, searching for anything that might burn.

By the time Ronny found her—he always seemed to know where she'd gone—Grace had swept a large area clean and built a small fire in the stove using broken chair legs and scraps of paper.

"What's this, then?" he asked, eyebrows raised as he surveyed her work.

"Our new home," Grace replied simply. "For now, at least."

Ronny grinned, revealing the gap where he'd lost a tooth in a scuffle months earlier. "I'll fetch the others."

Over the next few days, they transformed the abandoned mercantile. Grace directed their efforts with surprising authority, assigning tasks to each child according to their abilities.

Tom and Ronny repaired the door and secured loose boards over windows. Lizzie and Sarah swept away years of dust and grime. Even little Billy, no more than three, helped by collecting bits of coal that had spilled behind the old stove.

Grace felt a strange connection to the place, as if she were meant to find it. "It reminds me of stories my father told," she explained to Maggie, who'd come to inspect their new quarters. "About bringing light to dark places."

"You've certainly done that," the old flower seller observed, watching the children bustle about with purpose.

As Sunday approached, Grace had an idea. She recalled the church services her father had taken her to, how the familiar rituals had provided comfort even in their hardest times.

"We'll have our own service," she announced on Saturday evening. "Tomorrow morning, right here."

The children exchanged dubious glances.

"What for?" asked Tom, who'd never set foot in a church.

"To remember we're not alone," Grace replied. "To give thanks for this shelter and ask for protection."

When Sunday morning arrived, Grace woke early. She arranged broken crates as makeshift pews and placed her mother's prayer book on an upturned barrel at the front. The children filtered in gradually, their curiosity overcoming initial reluctance.

"Sit anywhere you like," Grace told them, her heart pounding with unexpected nervousness.

They settled on the floor, wrapped in whatever garments they possessed, eyes wide with anticipation. Several neighborhood children had joined them, drawn by Ronny's invitation and the promise of a warm place to sit for an hour.

Grace cleared her throat, suddenly unsure. What right had she to lead prayers? She was no vicar, just a girl with a tattered prayer book. But as she looked at the expectant faces before her—Ronny's encouraging nod, Lizzie's solemn attention, little Billy's thumb in his mouth—she felt a surge of certainty.

"My mother used to sing this hymn," she began, her voice soft but steady. "My father said it made the room feel warmer, even in the coldest winter."

Grace closed her eyes and began to sing, the familiar melody rising from somewhere deep within her:

"*Amazing grace, how sweet the sound,*
That saved a wretch like me.
I once was lost, but now am found,
Was blind, but now I see."

Her voice faltered on the high notes, but gained strength as Maggie's cracked alto joined in. By the second verse, several children were humming along, the shadowy room filling with their tentative music.

When the hymn ended, Grace opened her mother's prayer book to a well-worn page. "This is from Psalms," she explained. "My father read it to me when I was afraid."

She read slowly, letting the ancient words fill the dusty air: "The Lord is my shepherd; I shall not want. He maketh me to lie down in green pastures: he leadeth me beside the still waters."

The children listened, transfixed. Even the restless ones sat quietly, perhaps soothed by the rhythm of words they didn't fully understand but somehow felt.

After the reading, Grace invited them to share their own prayers. At first, no one spoke. Then Ronny cleared his throat.

"Thank you for this place," he said gruffly. "And for Angel Grace showing us the way here."

Others followed—halting, simple prayers for food, warmth, safety from the law. Little Billy asked God to help him find his lost marble. Grace felt tears prick her eyes at their earnestness.

When all who wished to speak had done so, Grace led them in the Lord's Prayer, which only a few knew. She taught them line by line, their voices joining hers with increasing confidence.

As they finished, a weak winter sun broke through the clouds, sending a shaft of light through a crack in the boarded windows. It illuminated the dusty air, creating a golden path across the room.

"Look," whispered Sarah. "It's like God is visiting."

Grace smiled, remembering her father's words about lamp-lighters bringing light to dark places. Perhaps this was her own way of continuing his work—not with a lamplighter's pole, but with her mother's prayers and her own determined spirit.

19
SUNDAY SERVICES

The next Sunday, Grace arrived at their makeshift sanctuary to find three unfamiliar faces—two boys and a girl with a bruised cheek—sitting nervously at the back.

"Ronny said we could come," the oldest boy explained, half-rising as if expecting to be sent away.

Grace smiled. "Everyone's welcome here."

Word travelled quickly through London's shadowy corners. Children whispered about the girl who offered prayers and comfort in an abandoned mercantile building, the one they called Angel Grace. By the third Sunday, their congregation had doubled. Some came for the stories, others for the brief respite from cold streets, but all found something they hadn't realised they were seeking.

"My mum used to tell me God forgot about us street folk," a hollow-cheeked girl named Martha confessed during their fourth gathering. "But when I'm here, I don't feel forgotten."

The services evolved beyond prayers and hymns. Children began sharing tales from their lives—some heartbreaking, others surprisingly funny. Laughter mingled with whispers of hope as they formed connections in a world that had discarded them.

"I reckon my dad's looking for me," Tommy announced one Sunday, his voice wavering between hope and doubt. "He promised he'd come back after finding work up north."

No one contradicted him, though several exchanged knowing glances. Grace squeezed his shoulder gently. "We'll keep watch for him," she promised, offering what comfort she could without crushing his fragile hope.

As winter's grip tightened, coughs and sniffles spread through their ranks. Grace's knowledge of remedies became as valuable as her prayers.

"This is yarrow," she explained one afternoon, showing a cluster of children the delicate white flowers she'd gathered from a neglected churchyard. "My mother used it for fevers and coughs."

She demonstrated how to prepare a simple tea, adding honey scavenged from the market's discarded combs. "The warmth helps as much as the herbs," she told them, watching as little Billy sipped cautiously before declaring it "not completely horrible."

Grace taught them which plants could ease stomach pains, which leaves reduced swelling when crushed and applied to bruises. She showed them how to make poultices for chests tight with winter coughs, using skills passed down from her mother through her father's memories.

"You're magic, Angel Grace," Sarah whispered one evening after Grace's mustard plaster eased her breathing.

Grace shook her head. "Not magic. Just knowledge that shouldn't be forgotten."

Their refuge became more than shelter from winter winds. Children brought whatever they could find—half-burnt candles, discarded blankets, occasionally even food. One memorable Sunday, Ronny arrived triumphant with a dented kettle and enough coal scraps for a small fire in the ancient stove.

"Where did you get those?" Grace asked suspiciously.

"Didn't steal 'em," he insisted. "Helped unload coal at the docks. Payment for honest work."

Grace chose to believe him, recognising the pride in his eyes at contributing something valuable.

The sharing of food became a ritual. No matter how meagre their offerings—bruised apples from the market floor, stale bread crusts, occasionally a bit of cheese—everything was divided equally.

"Like Jesus with the loaves and fishes," Grace explained, though their modest meals never miraculously multiplied.

"We ain't got much," Tom observed one Sunday, watching the careful division of a single meat pie someone had brought, "but it tastes better shared."

As January gave way to February, Grace found herself embracing a role she'd never anticipated. The children looked to her not just for prayers and remedies, but for guidance and reassurance.

"What happens when they tear this place down?" Lizzie asked one evening as they huddled around their small fire.

The question hung heavy in the air. Their sanctuary was temporary; they all knew it.

"Then we'll find another place," Grace answered firmly. "But more important than where we meet is that we stay together."

She looked around at their faces, illuminated by flickering flames. "We must promise to look after one another, no matter what comes. That's what families do."

"We ain't family," objected a newer boy whose name Grace hadn't yet learned. "Not by blood."

"Family's more than blood," Ronny countered. "It's who stands by you when the coppers come or when you're too sick to beg."

One by one, they nodded in agreement.

"Then let's make a pact," Grace suggested. "To help each other, to share what we have, to never leave anyone behind."

They joined hands in the firelight, a circle of children bound not by birth but by choice and circumstance. As Grace looked at their determined faces, she felt a resurgence of purpose igniting within her. This was her mother's legacy— not just healing bodies, but mending broken spirits and weaving love from the frayed threads of difficult lives.

The tranquility of their sanctuary didn't last. Grace first noticed the constable's interest one bitter Tuesday morning. She'd been selling matches near St Paul's when she spotted him—the same officer who'd chased Ronny last month— watching her from across the street, his gaze lingering longer than coincidence allowed.

"Keep your eyes sharp," Grace warned the children that evening. "They're taking notice of us."

The following Sunday, they gathered more cautiously. Grace positioned Lizzie as lookout near the broken window facing the street. Their hymns, normally sung with abandon, became hushed whispers that barely rose above the wind whistling through the building's gaps.

"Why must we hide?" asked Billy, his small face pinched with confusion. "We ain't doing nothing wrong."

Grace pulled him close. "Sometimes people fear what they don't understand. They see children without homes and think we're dangerous rather than just trying to survive."

Three days later, Grace overheard two officers talking as she pretended to arrange her matches near the tea shop.

"That abandoned mercantile on Porter Street—becoming a right den of thieves and vagrants," the taller one said. "Children running wild, no supervision. Commissioner wants it cleared by month's end."

"Nuisances, the lot of them," his companion agreed. "Frightening decent folk, driving down property values."

Grace's heart hammered against her ribs. Porter Street—their sanctuary. Their home.

That Sunday, she gathered everyone closer than usual, their breath visible in the frigid air despite their small fire.

"The police know about us," she announced, watching fear flicker across their faces. "They may come to drive us away."

Little Sarah began to cry silently. Tom's face hardened into a mask of defiance.

"We ain't leaving," Ronny declared. "This is ours now."

Grace shook her head gently. "The building isn't what matters. It's what we've built inside it—our faith, our trust in each other. That's what we take with us, wherever we go."

She opened her mother's prayer book, its pages still bearing water stains from the day the Hartwells cast her out.

"We've all weathered storms before," she reminded them, her voice steady despite her own fear. "We're strong enough to face this one together. We'll be more careful, meet at different times, post more lookouts—but we won't stop gathering."

The children nodded, their determination mirroring her own.

"Remember," Grace said softly, "light shines brightest in darkness."

20

WEATHERING THE STORM

The following Sunday brought a fearsome storm. Rain lashed against the warehouse walls, finding every crack and crevice. Wind howled through the broken windows, extinguishing two of their precious candles despite Grace's efforts to shield them.

"It sounds like the end of the world," whispered Sarah, her small body trembling.

Grace gathered the children closer, forming a tight circle on the floor. Little Billy climbed onto her lap while Ronny pressed against her side, trying to appear brave though his eyes betrayed his fear.

"Join hands," Grace instructed, her voice steady against the tempest outside. "When we stand together, no storm can truly harm us."

The children linked fingers—some grimy, some chapped from cold, all seeking connection. Grace felt Lizzie's hand trembling in her right palm, Tom's calloused grip in her left.

"Our Father, who watches over even the smallest sparrow," Grace began, not reciting from her prayer book but speaking from her heart, "guard these children through this storm. Give us courage to face whatever comes."

Thunder cracked directly overhead, causing several children to flinch. Billy buried his face against Grace's shoulder.

"We may not have sturdy walls," Grace continued, raising her voice above the din, "but we have something stronger—each other. Remember how Tom helped Lizzie when she was ill? How Ronny shared his bread when Sarah hadn't eaten? How Billy makes us laugh even on the coldest days?"

Nods circled through their huddle. The warehouse groaned under the assault of wind, but their circle held firm.

"That's how we survive—not alone, but together. The storm outside may rage, but in here, we have shelter in each other."

As if responding to her words, the children tightened their grip, forming an unbroken chain of small, determined hands. Grace felt their pulses against her palms—quick with fear but steady with trust. For a moment, the howling wind seemed distant, unable to penetrate the sanctuary they'd created not from brick and mortar, but from shared hardship and stubborn hope.

Two weeks later, Grace watched the children disperse after a particularly moving service. They'd sung "All Things Bright and Beautiful" with such enthusiasm that Grace worried they might attract attention, but the joy on their faces had been worth the risk.

She remained behind, gathering the stub of candle they'd used. In its dying glow, she surveyed their sanctuary—the barrel pulpit, the crates arranged as pews, the tattered blanket serving as an altar cloth. Such humble elements, yet they'd created something profound.

"Look at us now, Father," Grace whispered, touching the lamplighter's badge she kept wrapped in cloth. "We're still bringing light to dark places."

When the Hartwells had cast her out, Grace had believed everything lost. Yet here she stood, surrounded by evidence of renewal. Her mother's remedies eased suffering. Her father's stories comforted frightened children. Through her, their legacy continued.

Grace tucked her prayer book into her pocket and straightened the makeshift altar. She was no longer merely surviving—she was building something. These children looked to her not just for medicine or food, but for hope itself.

"Is this what you felt, Mother?" Grace asked the empty room. "This purpose?"

The candle flickered one last time before dying, but Grace didn't need its light to find her way. She'd become what her father once was—a lamplighter of sorts, illuminating paths through darkness. Not with gas and flame, but with faith and healing hands.

What once seemed an unbearable void—the loss of family, home, security—had transformed. Grace had filled that emptiness not by replacing what was lost, but by creating something entirely new: a family bound not by blood but by choice, a home carried within rather than built of brick, and security found in mutual care rather than locks and doors.

The Sunday services flourished beyond Grace's initial vision. What began as her solitary mission evolved organically as others found their voices. Lizzie, with her surprising memory for hymns, began leading the singing. Tom, though quiet in daily life, revealed a gift for storytelling, bringing Bible parables to life with animated gestures that captivated even the youngest children.

On mornings when Grace was called away to tend to Old Maggie's worsening cough or deliver remedies to dock workers struck with fever, the services continued without pause. Ronny, once the most skeptical among them, now stood before the barrel pulpit with surprising authority, his rough voice softening as he recited passages Grace had taught him. The children no longer waited for Grace's guidance to begin—they arranged the crates, lit the candles, and passed around whatever meagre offerings they'd gathered that week. Grace watched this transformation with quiet pride, understanding that true sanctuary wasn't built by a single keeper of the flame, but by many hands holding their small lights together, creating something brighter than any could maintain alone.

21

COLLAPSE

A biting wind howled through London's streets, tearing at Grace's threadbare shawl as if determined to strip away her last defence against winter's fury. She stumbled forward, one foot before the other, each step heavier than the last. Nineteen winters she'd weathered, but none so cruel as this.

"Just... keep moving," Grace murmured, her cracked lips barely forming the words.

The wind cut through her like glass. Grace clutched her mother's prayer book tighter to her chest, its familiar weight both comfort and burden. Snow gathered in drifts against buildings, pristine white mocking the grey pallor of her skin.

"St Bartholomew's... just round the corner," she whispered, though no one walked beside her. The mission offered soup on Tuesdays. Was it Tuesday? The days had blurred together in a haze of hunger and cold.

Grace's vision swam. Buildings tilted at impossible angles. Her fingers, numb and blue-tinged, fumbled for her locket chain, tangling desperately in its links. Mary Hartwell's portrait lay inside, a mother's face Grace knew only through her father's stories and her own imagination.

"Mother, I've tried ... to be like you."

Her knees buckled. The world tilted. Grace felt herself falling but lacked the strength to catch herself. The snow rushed up to meet her, surprisingly soft against her cheek. Not so cold, after all. Almost warm.

The stone steps of St Bartholomew's Mission pressed against her side. So close. Just a few more steps would have brought her to help, to warmth. Grace's fingers remained tangled in the locket chain, her mother's prayer book clutched against her heart.

Darkness edged her vision. Snowflakes melted against her feverish forehead. Grace thought of Ronny, of Billy and Lizzie —who would care for them now? Who would remember her father's stories? Her mother's remedies?

The mission door opened, spilling golden light across the snow. A man's voice called out. Footsteps crunched toward her. But Grace heard nothing as consciousness slipped away, her world fading to blessed, painless black.

22

DOCTOR COULSON

"Quickly now! This poor girl's half frozen."

Hands lifted Grace from the snow-laden steps, carrying her through the doorway into St Bartholomew's Mission. The sudden warmth prickled her skin like needles, though she remained unconscious, her body limp as they laid her on a narrow cot in the clinic area.

"She's dangerously cold. Fetch more blankets—the woollen ones from the back cupboard." The voice belonged to a young man, authoritative yet tinged with genuine concern. "And prepare hot water for tea. Willow bark and ginger, if we have it."

Through the fog of unconsciousness, Grace sensed movement around her. Someone removed her sodden boots and wrapped her feet in dry cloth. Another placed heated bricks near her body, their warmth seeping slowly into her frozen limbs.

"Doctor Coulson, her fingers—they're blue at the tips."

"Warm them gradually. Too much heat too quickly could

damage the tissue." The doctor's hands were gentle as they examined her. "She's clutching something... a book and a necklace. Don't remove them; they seem important to her."

A woman's voice joined the conversation. "Poor lamb. She's naught but skin and bones."

"She's been starving for some time," the doctor agreed, his voice dropping lower. "But there's something about her ... look how clean her clothes are despite their condition. She's taken care with what little she has."

Time passed in strange ebbs and flows. Grace drifted between darkness and hazy awareness, catching fragments of conversation, feeling hands adjusting blankets, sensing the gradual return of warmth to her body.

"Her colour's improving, Doctor."

"Good. Keep the tea ready. She'll need it when she wakes."

Grace's eyelids fluttered. The ceiling above her came into focus—wooden beams illuminated by soft candlelight. She blinked slowly, awareness returning in small waves. The prayer book remained clutched against her chest, her fingers still entwined in the locket chain.

She turned her head slightly, wincing at the effort. A young man sat beside her cot, writing notes in a small book. His face, framed by the gentle glow of candlelight, was handsome—kind eyes, strong jaw, dark hair falling slightly across his forehead. He couldn't be much older than she was.

He looked up, noticing her movement, and smiled.

"You're awake. That's excellent." He set aside his notes and leaned closer. "You gave us quite a fright, collapsing on our doorstep like that."

Grace tried to speak, but her throat felt raw, her voice emerging as little more than a whisper. "Thank ... you."

Despite her weakness, she managed a fragile smile, fingers

tightening around her mother's prayer book. The simple act of holding it grounded her, connecting her to a past that seemed increasingly distant.

"I'm Doctor Edmund Coulson." He poured tea from a pitcher into a cup. "Can you sit up a little? You need to drink this."

With his help, Grace managed to raise herself slightly. The tea was warm and sweet, soothing her parched throat.

"Grace," she whispered after drinking. "My name is Grace Hartwell."

"Miss Hartwell." He nodded, studying her face with an intensity that might have made her uncomfortable had it not been so clearly born of concern rather than judgment. "You're safe now. We'll help you recover your strength."

"The children," Grace suddenly remembered, attempting to sit up further. "Ronny and the others—they'll be worried."

Edmund gently pressed her shoulder, easing her back down. "You're in no condition to go anywhere tonight. Your friends will have to manage until you're stronger."

Grace reluctantly settled back, knowing he was right. Her eyes met his, finding unexpected warmth there. Despite her circumstances—despite being a street girl in a charity mission —he spoke to her with respect, as if she mattered.

"That book," Edmund nodded toward the prayer book still clutched in her hands. "It must be precious to you."

"It was my mother's." Grace's voice strengthened slightly. "And my father's before ... before the fog took him."

Something in Edmund's expression shifted—a flicker of interest beyond professional concern. "Rest now, Miss Hartwell. We can talk more tomorrow."

As exhaustion pulled her back toward sleep, Grace watched the young doctor through half-closed eyes. His movements were precise yet gentle as he checked her pulse, his face a study in compassion. In her last moments of wakefulness, she wondered at the strange twist of fate that had brought her to this place, to this man's care.

23
A NEW MISSION

Morning light streamed through the small window of the mission's infirmary as Grace awoke. Her body ached less, and the warmth of blankets no longer felt foreign against her skin. She sat up carefully, surveying the room. Several other beds lined the walls, most occupied by figures curled beneath threadbare blankets.

"Good morning, Miss Hartwell." Doctor Coulson appeared at her bedside, his smile genuine. "You're looking considerably better today."

"I feel it," Grace admitted, though her voice remained hoarse. "Thank you for your kindness."

He checked her pulse, his touch professional yet gentle. "Your fever's broken. That's excellent progress."

Over the next several days, Edmund visited her frequently, often lingering longer than his duties required. Grace noticed how he spoke to her—not with the condescending pity common among charitable workers, but with genuine interest. He asked about her life before the streets, listening intently as she shared fragments of her story.

"My father was a lamplighter," she told him on the third day, sitting propped against pillows. "We lived above Grigson's Bakery in Whitechapel. It wasn't much, but it was home."

Edmund pulled a chair closer. "And your mother? You mentioned her prayer book."

Grace's fingers traced the worn leather cover. "She died bringing me into the world. But Father spoke of her every day —her kindness, her singing, her knowledge of healing herbs." A wistful smile crossed her face. "He taught me everything he remembered about her remedies. Said I had her gift."

"Is that so?" Edmund leaned forward, curiosity brightening his eyes. "What sort of remedies?"

"Simple things, mostly. Yarrow for fevers, comfrey for bruises, willow bark for pain." She shrugged. "Nothing a proper doctor would find impressive."

"On the contrary," Edmund replied. "There's wisdom in traditional knowledge that medical schools often overlook."

On the fifth day, Edmund arrived carrying a small wooden box. "I've brought something that might interest you." He set it on her bed, opening the lid to reveal several bundles of dried herbs.

Grace's eyes widened. Without hesitation, she reached for a sprig of dried leaves. "Feverfew," she identified, bringing it to her nose. "Excellent for headaches, especially when brewed with a touch of mint."

Edmund watched, astonished, as she sorted through the collection, naming each herb and its uses without faltering.

"This elderflower would work better if harvested earlier in the season," she noted, examining a bundle. "And this valerian —it's perfect for sleeplessness, but bitter. I usually add honey when making it for children."

"Children?" Edmund raised an eyebrow.

Grace's expression shifted, sudden concern flooding her

features. "The children—my children—I mean, not mine, but ..." She clutched at the blanket. "Ronny and the others. They'll be looking for me. They need me."

Edmund placed a reassuring hand over hers. "Tell me about them."

The words poured out—stories of Ronny's fierce protectiveness, little Billy's persistent cough, Lizzie's talent for singing, Tom's quiet strength. Grace described their Sunday gatherings, how they'd transformed an abandoned warehouse into a sanctuary of sorts.

"They have no one else," she finished, tears gathering in her eyes. "I promised I'd look after them."

Edmund considered her words, then nodded decisively. "I will send some people out to find them. Perhaps we could organise regular visits to your warehouse—bring food, blankets, medicines."

"You would do that?" Grace asked, hardly daring to believe.

"Of course." His smile reached his eyes. "The mission's purpose is to help those in need, not just those who find their way to our door."

As days passed and Grace's strength returned, Edmund began bringing her small tasks—sorting herbs, preparing simple tinctures. Their conversations flowed easily, moving between medical discussions and personal stories. Grace shared tales of her father's lamplighting rounds, while Edmund spoke of his training at medical school and his decision to volunteer at the mission despite his family's reservations.

A week after Grace's collapse, the mission doors burst open during breakfast, bringing a rush of cold air and urgent voices. Grace looked up from her porridge to see Ronny barrelling through the dining hall, his face flushed from running, with Tom, Lizzie, and little Billy trailing behind.

"Grace!" Ronny shouted, ignoring the startled looks from mission staff. He skidded to a halt at her table. "We thought you was dead!"

Grace rose unsteadily, her legs still weak. "I'm alive, just a bit poorly." She opened her arms and the children surged forward, enveloping her in a tangle of bony limbs and unwashed clothes.

Billy buried his face in her skirt. "Angel Grace, we looked everywhere."

"Doctor Coulson found me." Grace smoothed Billy's matted hair. "He's been taking care of me."

Edmund appeared in the doorway, watching the reunion with a smile. He approached with measured steps. "This must be your family."

Ronny squared his shoulders, eyeing Edmund suspiciously. "Who's he, then?"

"This is Doctor Coulson," Grace explained. "He saved my life."

Edmund crouched to Billy's level. "You must be Billy. Grace told me about your cough." He produced a small bottle from his pocket. "Three drops in water, morning and night."

Billy accepted the bottle with wide eyes.

"I've arranged something," Edmund told Grace. "The mission will provide a hot meal each day for any child who comes. Mrs Pinkerton has gathered clothes—proper winter clothes—and we've medicine for those who need it."

Tears welled in Grace's eyes. "I don't know how to thank you."

"There's more," Edmund continued. "Two of our volunteers will visit your warehouse weekly. They'll bring food, clothes, and check on anyone who's ill."

Ronny's suspicion melted slightly. "Why would you do all that?"

"Because that is what we're here for. That is our mission." Edmund replied simply.

Over the following days, the children returned daily. They arrived wary but left with full bellies and bundles of necessities. Grace watched with swelling pride as Lizzie helped distribute blankets, Tom carried coal for elderly mission workers, and even Ronny grudgingly assisted in the kitchen.

"They're good children," Grace told Edmund as they sorted donated clothing together. "They just needed someone to care."

Edmund's hands paused over a small woollen coat. "They're fortunate to have you." His voice carried a warmth that made Grace's cheeks flush. "As are we. Your knowledge of remedies has already improved our treatments considerably."

Grace ducked her head, focusing on folding a scarf. "I'm the fortunate one."

By the second week, Grace was well enough to assist with other patients. Edmund watched with admiration as she coaxed a reluctant child into taking medicine, her gentle manner more effective than his medical authority.

"You have a gift," he told her one evening as they worked side by side, preparing herbal remedies for the next day. "Not just knowledge of herbs, but understanding of people."

Grace laughed softly. "Living on the streets teaches you to read people quickly. It's a matter of survival."

"Yet you've maintained such compassion." Edmund measured dried chamomile into small packets. "Many in your position would have grown bitter."

"What good would bitterness do?" She shrugged. "My father always said that even in darkness, we must carry our own light."

Edmund paused, studying her face in the lamplight. "Your father sounds like he was a wise man."

"He was." Grace smiled, a memory surfacing. "Once, during a terrible storm, he took me on his rounds anyway. I was frightened of the thunder, so he told me the most ridiculous stories about the clouds having arguments. By the end, I was laughing so hard I forgot to be afraid."

Her laughter filled the small workroom, bright and unexpected. Edmund found himself joining in, struck by how natural it felt to share this moment with her.

Later, as they finished their work, Edmund gathered courage to ask, "Would you consider staying on here, Miss Hartwell? Not just as a patient, but as an assistant of sorts. Your knowledge of herbal remedies could be invaluable."

Grace looked up, surprise evident in her expression. "You would want my help? But I'm not trained. I'm just—"

"You're just Grace Hartwell," Edmund interrupted gently, "who knows more about healing herbs than most physicians I've met, who cares deeply for those that others have forgotten, and who somehow maintains hope despite everything you've endured."

In the quiet that followed, something shifted between them—an unspoken recognition that their connection had grown beyond doctor and patient, beyond even colleagues. Grace felt it in the warmth spreading through her chest, saw it in the way Edmund's eyes held hers a moment longer than necessary.

"I would be honoured to help," she finally said, her voice soft but steady. "Thank you for seeing value in what I can offer."

Edmund smiled, and in that smile Grace glimpsed possibilities she had never dared imagine—a future where her knowledge was respected, where her care for others could become her purpose rather than merely her survival.

24
A ROOM OF HER OWN

Grace stood outside a modest boarding house on Barlow Street, her heart racing with a mix of excitement and trepidation. The sign above the door read "Rooms for Rent" in faded black lettering. She clutched her worn shawl tighter around her shoulders, drawing a deep breath before approaching the entrance.

The door opened before she could knock, revealing an elderly woman with silver-streaked hair and kind eyes.

"Looking for a room, are you, dear?" The woman's gaze swept over Grace, taking in her clean but mended dress and the determined set of her jaw.

"Yes, ma'am. If you please."

"I'm Mrs Browne. Come in before you catch your death." She ushered Grace into a narrow hallway that smelled of beeswax and fresh bread. "You've the look of someone who's seen harder times than most."

Grace tensed, wondering if this would lead to rejection, but Mrs Browne's expression held no judgment—only understanding.

"I work at St Bartholomew's Mission now," Grace explained. "With Doctor Coulson. I assist with the patients and prepare herbal remedies."

Mrs Browne nodded approvingly. "Honest work, that. Come, I've a room on the upper floor. Small, but it catches the morning light."

The room was indeed small—barely space for a narrow bed, a chest of drawers, and a chair beneath the window. But the floors were clean, the bedding fresh, and the window over-looked a small courtyard where a scraggly apple tree stretched toward the sky.

"It's perfect," Grace whispered, imagining waking to sunlight rather than the damp chill of warehouse corners or the suffocating darkness of the Hartwells' attic.

"Six shillings weekly, includes breakfast," Mrs Browne said. "Need first payment in advance."

Grace's heart sank. She'd been saving her small earnings from the mission, but hadn't accumulated enough yet. "I understand. Perhaps in another week—"

"I'll hold it three days," Mrs Browne offered. "No longer, mind. Too many looking for decent lodgings these days."

The next afternoon, Grace shared her dilemma with Edmund as they sorted through a new shipment of supplies at the mission.

"It's a lovely room," she explained, measuring dried chamomile into paper packets. "Mrs Browne seems fair, and it's close enough to walk here each day. I just need another week to save enough for the first payment."

Edmund paused in his inventory, watching her method-ical movements. "This boarding house—it's on Barlow Street?"

"Yes. Do you know it?"

"I've heard it's respectable. Mrs Browne has a reputation

for running a clean, orderly house." He hesitated. "Grace, I could help with the first payment."

Her hands stilled. "I couldn't possibly—"

"Consider it an advance on your wages," he said quickly. "You've more than earned it with your work here."

Grace looked up, meeting his earnest gaze. Warmth bloomed in her chest, followed immediately by worry. What would people think, a doctor helping a former street girl? What would he expect in return?

Yet Edmund's eyes held nothing but genuine kindness.

"I don't know how to thank you," she said finally.

"Your continued assistance here is thanks enough." His smile reached his eyes. "Everyone deserves a safe place to call home."

Two days later, Grace stood in the centre of her new room, scarcely believing it belonged to her. She placed her mother's prayer book on the windowsill where morning light would touch its worn cover. From her pocket, she withdrew three wildflowers she'd purchased with a farthing at the market—simple daisies, but they brightened the room when placed in a chipped cup filled with water.

Each morning, Grace rose early to help Mrs Browne with breakfast preparations before walking to the mission. Her days fell into a rhythm—mixing remedies, tending to patients, and visiting the warehouse to check on Ronny and the others. In the evenings, she returned to her room, often bringing bits of medicinal herbs to dry on her windowsill.

On Sundays, she still led services at the warehouse, though now she could offer more than prayers—she brought food purchased with her small wages and remedies prepared at the mission.

Each night, Grace carefully counted her coins, setting aside the exact amount needed for next week's rent. The responsibility weighed heavily, yet filled her with quiet pride. For the first time since her father's death, she had a place that felt truly hers—a sanctuary where she could close the door and breathe freely.

25
PARTNERS IN HEALING

"It was Billy who found the old kettle," Grace said, carefully wrapping a poultice around Mrs Winters' swollen wrist. "Cracked, of course, but Ronny managed to seal it with candle wax. That night we had proper tea for everyone."

Edmund leaned against the mission's dispensary counter, captivated by her story. "And where did the tea come from?"

"Old Maggie—the flower seller. She had save her tea leaves, dry them again on newspaper. Not as strong the second time, but still warm." Grace secured the bandage with practiced fingers. "There you are, Mrs Winters. Keep it dry and come back tomorrow."

The elderly woman examined her wrist with appreciation. "Bless you, dearie. The pain's eased already."

After Mrs Winters departed, Edmund shook his head in wonder. "I've never heard of reusing tea leaves."

"When you have nothing, you waste nothing." Grace began tidying the workbench. "The streets teach resourcefulness. Like how the bakers near Covent Garden leave their day-old bread in sacks behind their shops instead of locking it away.

They pretend not to notice when children collect it after midnight."

"Deliberate charity disguised as carelessness," Edmund mused.

"Exactly." Grace smiled. "Or how Mrs Finch at the laundry leaves her clothesline accessible so street children can take a single item when truly desperate. Never more—there's honour among us. Take one shirt when you're soaked to the bone, but leave the rest."

Edmund's expression softened. "I've walked these streets my entire life without seeing any of this."

"It's not meant to be seen by those who don't need to see it." Grace sorted dried herbs into glass jars. "The watchman on Fleet Street who warns children when inspectors are coming. The publican's wife who leaves buckets of clean water by her back door. Small kindnesses that mean everything."

Edmund was quiet for a moment. "At medical school, we studied disease and anatomy, but never how people actually survive."

"Perhaps that's why your treatments sometimes fail where they shouldn't," Grace suggested gently. "You heal bodies but forget that bodies house spirits that need nurturing too."

The following Tuesday, Edmund arrived at the mission clutching a stack of leather-bound journals, his eyes bright with excitement.

"I've brought something," he announced, laying them carefully on the table. "Medical journals from Edinburgh. There are fascinating new approaches to treatment that might complement your herbal remedies."

Grace wiped her hands on her apron, drawn to the scholarly volumes. "May I?"

"They're for you to read," Edmund said, opening the top journal to a marked page. "This one discusses the healing properties of willow bark—something you've mentioned using. The author theorises about the specific compounds that reduce fever and pain."

Grace leaned closer, her fingers tracing the elegant diagrams. "This explains why it works better when steeped longer. I've noticed that, but never understood why."

Edmund turned to another journal. "And here—research on treating infections with moulds. It reminded me of your poultice for Mrs Tenney's infected cut."

"Bread mould mixed with honey," Grace nodded. "My mother taught my father that remedy. I never questioned why it worked."

They spent the afternoon poring over the journals, Edmund explaining medical terminology while Grace connected theories to her practical experience. When Sister Agnes announced the mission was closing for the evening, they were still deep in conversation.

"We could try combining your willow bark tea with proper dosing schedules," Edmund suggested as they gathered the journals. "Perhaps record the results systematically."

"And add meadowsweet for stomach protection," Grace added. "The willow can be harsh on empty stomachs."

The next week brought opportunities to test their ideas. A dock worker arrived with a badly sprained ankle. Edmund examined him, then glanced at Grace.

"What would you suggest?"

Grace stepped forward confidently. "Cold compresses first, then a poultice of comfrey and arnica. But we should also immobilize it as you've shown me, with proper bandaging."

Edmund nodded approvingly. "And for the pain?"

"Willow bark tea, prepared as we discussed—steeped exactly fifteen minutes and administered every four hours."

Their combined approach yielded remarkable results. The

dock worker returned two days later, astonished by his improvement.

"Whatever you did, it's working better than anything I've tried before," he told them. "The swelling's nearly gone."

Word spread quickly. More patients arrived at the mission, seeking the care of "the doctor and his herb girl." Each success strengthened their partnership, with Grace growing more confident in sharing her knowledge and Edmund increasingly valuing her intuitive understanding.

"We make quite the team," Edmund remarked one evening as they reviewed their day's work.

Grace looked up from her notes, a smile illuminating her face. "It's like we're bringing together two worlds that should never have been separated."

"Medicine and nature," Edmund agreed. "Science and tradition."

"Doctor and street girl," Grace added softly.

Edmund's eyes met hers, holding her gaze a moment longer than necessary. "No," he said firmly. "Colleagues. Partners in healing."

26

A SHARED VISION

Candles flickered across the mission's dispensary, casting long shadows as Grace and Edmund laboured well past closing time. Outside, London's streets had grown quiet, but inside, their conversation bubbled with enthusiasm. They'd spent hours treating a seemingly endless queue of patients—dock workers with mangled hands, laundresses with scalded arms, children with hacking coughs.

"We turned away twelve people today," Grace said, scrubbing dried herbs from beneath her fingernails. "Mrs Fenwick's arthritis will only worsen without treatment."

Edmund sighed, loosening his collar. "And the Hatcher children's mother. Her cough sounded dreadful."

"Consumption, I'd wager." Grace's voice dropped. "I've seen it before. The mission simply hasn't enough beds."

"Or time." Edmund leaned against the wooden counter, exhaustion evident in the slump of his shoulders. "Or space. Or supplies."

Grace paused her cleaning, struck by a thought that had been forming in her mind for weeks. She reached for her worn notebook—once her remedy journal, now filled with patient notes and treatment combinations.

"What if we had our own place?" The words tumbled out before she could reconsider their boldness. "Not grand, mind you. Just... ours."

Edmund's eyebrows lifted. "A clinic, you mean?"

"A proper healing place." Grace flipped to a blank page and began sketching with quick, decisive strokes. "With shelves for my herbs alongside your medicines. Windows for light and fresh air. Perhaps a small garden in the back for growing what we need."

Edmund moved beside her, watching as the vision took shape on paper. His shoulder brushed against hers, but neither moved away.

"It would need examination rooms," he contributed. "At least two."

"And a waiting area where people needn't stand in the rain." Grace's pencil moved faster. "With benches, not church pews that make backs ache."

"Books," Edmund added. "Medical texts, but also information people can understand about their own bodies."

"Tea always available." Grace smiled. "Simple comforts matter when you're ill."

The sketch grew more detailed—a modest building with practical rooms, nothing fancy but welcoming to all. Grace added little touches: herb bundles hanging from rafters, a kettle perpetually steaming, wide doorways for those who struggled to walk.

"We'd treat everyone," she said softly. "Not just those who can pay."

"But those who can would help support those who can't," Edmund reasoned. "A sliding scale of fees, perhaps."

"And we'd listen." Grace's pencil stilled. "Truly listen. Not rushing people through like cattle."

Edmund's finger traced the outline of her drawing. "You've thought about this."

"I dream of it," she admitted. "A place where healing comes from both your learning and my mother's wisdom. Where dock workers and bankers sit side by side, treated with equal dignity."

"Where science and tradition complement rather than compete," Edmund murmured.

The candles guttered as a draft swept through the room, but neither noticed. They bent over the notebook, adding details, debating practicalities, building their shared vision stroke by stroke.

"It would need a name," Edmund said.

"Something simple. Honest." Grace tapped her pencil against her lip. "Coulson and Hartwell Healing Rooms."

Edmund's smile reached his eyes. "Hartwell and Coulson, surely?"

"Alphabetical order," Grace retorted with a laugh.

The night deepened around them, but they remained absorbed in their creation, their voices mingling in the candle-light. Grace felt something unfamiliar bloom in her chest—not just hope, but possibility. For the first time since her father's death, she could envision a future that wasn't merely survival but purpose.

"We could do this," Edmund whispered, as if afraid to break the spell. "Truly, we could."

Grace nodded, unable to speak past the lump in her throat. Their dream lay before them, sketched in pencil but vivid in their minds—a shared vision that bound their hearts together more surely than any formal agreement.

EDMUND STEPPED out into the cool night air, his medical bag swinging lightly at his side. The streets of London lay quiet around him, most respectable folk tucked safely in their beds. His mind, however, was anything but quiet—it raced with sketches of examination rooms, herb shelves, and Grace's face illuminated by candlelight as she'd shared her vision.

He took the long way home, past shuttered shops and darkened windows. The gentle tap of his boots against cobblestones echoed his heartbeat—steady but quickening whenever he thought of Grace's clever hands sorting herbs, or the determined set of her jaw when she argued for a patient's needs.

"Coulson and Hartwell," he murmured, testing the sound of it. "Hartwell and Coulson."

Either way, it felt right. Natural. As if their names belonged together.

A carriage rumbled past, splashing through a puddle. Edmund sidestepped it neatly, his thoughts returning to his father's study—that imposing room with its leather-bound medical texts and framed credentials. He could almost smell the pipe tobacco and beeswax polish, hear his father's measured voice.

"A physician of your calibre belongs on Harley Street, Edmund. Not frittering away your talents among the destitute."

Edmund had nodded then, as he always did. The path had seemed clear enough—complete his training, establish a practice among people who could afford his services, marry a suitable young woman from their circle. Perhaps Miss Ashford, whose father had made his fortune in shipping and whose dowry would furnish a handsome practice indeed.

He paused at a crossroads, looking down one street toward Mayfair, where his rented rooms awaited, and down another toward the river, where Grace's boarding house stood. Two directions. Two futures.

The practical voice in his head—the one that sounded remarkably like his father—listed all the sensible objections. Grace had no family connections, no fortune, and no formal education. She'd lived on the streets. What would his mother say? What would his colleagues think?

Yet when he closed his eyes, he saw Grace bending over a feverish child, her touch gentle but sure. He heard her voice explaining the properties of herbs with such natural authority that even the most sceptical patients listened. He remembered how she'd recognised the pain behind Mrs Collins' complaints when he'd nearly dismissed the woman as merely difficult.

"She heals differently than I do," he whispered to the empty street. "But no less effectively."

Edmund resumed walking toward Mayfair, his stride purposeful. His father had plans—had always had plans. The Coulson name carried weight in medical circles, built on generations of respectable practice among respectable people. To throw that away for a clinic in some unfashionable district, alongside a woman with no credentials beyond her remarkable intuition and knowledge ...

Yet something in him had shifted. The mission work his father dismissed as "charitable indulgence" had become more than duty—it had become purpose. The people Grace championed weren't abstract notions of "the poor" but individuals with names and stories and dignity.

Edmund reached his door and paused, key in hand. Two paths stretched before him—the expected and the extraordinary. One safe, one uncertain.

He thought of Grace's face as she'd sketched their clinic, how alive she'd looked, how right it had felt to stand beside her.

The choice, he realised, had already been made.

27
A CHANCE

Grace sat by the mission's window, watching the winter night sky. Frost had etched delicate patterns across the glass, like nature's own lace curtains. Beyond them, stars punctured the darkness with brilliant clarity, each one a pinprick of light against London's vast blackness.

Her mother's prayer book rested in her lap, its worn leather smooth beneath her fingertips. She traced the faded gold lettering, remembering how her father would read from it by candlelight, his voice steady and comforting in their small room above Grigson's Bakery.

"Look at those stars, Grace," he'd once told her. "Even on the darkest night, they're still there, guiding the way."

How far she'd come since those days. From the cold attic in the Hartwell household where Agatha's harsh words had cut deeper than winter winds. From doorways where she'd huddled against the rain, her stomach twisted with hunger. From the warehouse where she'd gathered children around her, sharing what little she had.

Now she had a room of her own at Mrs Browne's. A position at the mission. And Edmund.

Edmund, with his gentle hands and thoughtful questions. Edmund, who looked at her as if she were something precious, not something broken.

Grace closed her eyes, allowing herself to imagine what could be. A proper clinic with windows that let in sunlight. Shelves lined with herbs and tinctures. People coming for help and leaving with hope. A small cottage perhaps, with a garden where she could grow healing plants. A place where she belonged.

And Edmund beside her through it all.

Her eyes snapped open. The vision scattered like startled birds.

What foolishness. The voice in her head sounded suspiciously like Agatha Hartwell's. A street girl dreaming of a doctor's love? Mind your place, girl.

Grace pressed her palm against the cold window, feeling the bite of winter through the glass. Tomorrow she would walk through the market and see ladies in fine dresses, their hands soft and callous free, their speech refined. They would glance at her—if they noticed her at all—and see someone beneath them.

Someone like Edmund belonged with them, not with her.

"You're still awake."

Edmund's voice startled her. He stood in the doorway, a steaming cup in each hand.

"I brought tea," he said, crossing to join her. "You looked cold."

Grace accepted the cup, warming her hands around it. "Thank you."

Edmund settled into the chair opposite, his gaze following

hers to the night sky. "Beautiful, isn't it? Makes one feel rather small."

"And rather insignificant," Grace murmured.

Edmund's brow furrowed. "Is that how you feel?"

Grace sipped her tea, buying time. "Sometimes. Don't you? All those grand houses in Mayfair, all those important people making decisions that affect the rest of us—they seem to inhabit a different world entirely."

"A different world, perhaps. Not a better one." Edmund leaned forward. "Do you know what I observed today? Mrs Finchley—you remember, the banker's wife with the persistent headaches—she couldn't tell me which of her children had the measles last year. Her nursemaid had handled it entirely."

Grace frowned. "But surely—"

"Meanwhile, I watched you with the Cooper family. You remembered not just Tommy's fever from last month, but that his sister had been frightened of the medicine, that their mother works at the laundry on Tuesdays, and that their father's cough worsens when he works the night shift."

Heat crept into Grace's cheeks. "That's just—"

"That's not just anything, Grace. That's seeing people. Really seeing them." Edmund set his cup down. "Those fine ladies in their silk dresses? Most of them have never truly see the people around them. You have. And that makes you a better healer than half the physicians I trained with."

Grace looked down at her hands—clean now, but still bearing calluses from years of scrubbing floors and washing laundry. Hands that had known work and pain and healing.

"When I was on the streets," she said quietly, "there was a woman who sold flowers near Covent Garden. Every day, hundreds of people walked past her. But she told me most never looked at her face—she was just the flower seller, not a person with hopes and dreams and sorrows."

Edmund nodded. "And you?"

"I always looked at her face. I knew when her joints pained her in the damp. I knew which days her son had visited and which days he hadn't." Grace smiled faintly. "She gave me daisies once, said I was the only one who saw her."

"That's what I mean." Edmund's voice was warm. "Your past isn't something to overcome, Grace. It's what makes you extraordinary."

Grace stared at him, this man who seemed to see past every barrier she'd built. "The world doesn't work that way, Edmund. People like me don't—"

"People like you," he interrupted gently, "change the world when given half a chance."

His words wrapped around her like a blanket, muffling the harsh voices of doubt. For one precious moment, Grace allowed herself to believe him—to see herself through his eyes.

"Our clinic," she whispered, testing the words. "Do you really think we could?"

Edmund's smile was like sunrise. "I've never been more certain of anything."

28
LEGACY

E dmund entered his family's townhouse with Grace's words still warming his heart. The grand entrance hall, with its polished marble and gleaming brass, felt hollow compared to the simple mission dispensary where they'd sketched their dreams.

"Edmund, darling! We'd nearly given up on you." His mother swept into the hall, her silk dress rustling. Lady Coulson's carefully arranged silver hair and pearl earrings marked her as firmly part of London's respectable society. "Your father's been asking after you all evening."

"Clinic matters, Mother." Edmund removed his coat, handing it to the waiting butler. "We had several difficult cases today."

"That dreadful place." She sighed, taking his arm as they walked toward the drawing room. "I do wish you'd spend more time at Dr Pembroke's practice. Much more suitable connections to be made there."

Edmund tensed. "The mission serves those who need help most."

"Yes, yes, very charitable." She patted his hand. "But charity work is for Sundays, dear. Your future requires proper attention."

Dr. Reginald Coulson stood by the fireplace, brandy in hand. His imposing figure and stern expression had intimidated generations of medical students.

"There you are, boy. Punctuality still escapes you, I see."

"Father." Edmund nodded respectfully. "I apologise for the delay. We had—"

"—patients at that mission, yes." His father waved away the explanation. "I've heard concerning reports about you, Edmund."

Edmund's stomach tightened. "Reports?"

"Mrs Finchley mentioned seeing you walking with some girl from the mission. Apparently quite familiar with each other." His father's gaze was penetrating. "She described the girl as looking... respectable enough, but clearly not of our circle."

"Grace Hartwell is my assistant at the dispensary." Edmund kept his voice level. "She has remarkable knowledge of herbal remedies."

"An assistant?" His mother looked relieved. "Well, that's perfectly appropriate then."

"Is it merely professional, Edmund?" His father pressed. "Because Frederick Pembroke saw you dining with her at that little café near St Bartholomew's. Said you looked rather ... engaged in conversation."

Heat rose in Edmund's face. "Grace is intelligent and compassionate. Her insights have helped countless patients."

"Edmund." His mother's voice sharpened. "You cannot possibly be forming an attachment to this ... this dispensary girl?"

"Her name is Grace," Edmund said firmly. "And yes, I admire her greatly."

The silence that followed was deafening. His mother sank onto a chair, hand fluttering to her throat. His father set down his glass with deliberate care.

"This is absurd." Dr Coulson's voice was dangerously quiet. "You've been raised for better things, Edmund. A respected practice. A suitable marriage. Not some infatuation with a girl from the streets."

"She's not just—"

"Do you have any idea what this would do to your prospects?" His father continued. "To our family name? To everything we've built?"

His mother dabbed at her eyes with a handkerchief. "Think of poor Millicent Bashford. Her father has all but announced your understanding."

"There is no understanding with Millicent," Edmund said firmly. "We've barely exchanged ten words."

"She's perfectly suitable," his mother insisted. "Beautiful, accomplished, from an excellent family. Her father's connections alone would secure your practice for life."

Edmund paced the room, frustration building. "And what of happiness? What of finding someone whose mind challenges mine, whose heart matches my own?"

"Romantic nonsense." His father dismissed with a wave. "Marriage is a practical arrangement, Edmund. You'll find contentment in shared values and position."

"Grace shares my values far more than Millicent ever could."

His mother gasped. "You cannot be serious. A girl with no family, no education, no standing—"

"She has all three," Edmund countered. "Her father was a lamplighter, her mother a healer. She's educated herself despite impossible circumstances. And her standing? She's earned the respect of everyone at the mission through her own merit."

"Enough!" His father thundered. "This conversation is finished. You will end this inappropriate attachment immediately. Your future is too important to throw away on some passing fancy."

Edmund straightened his shoulders. "Grace is not a passing fancy."

"Then you're a greater fool than I thought." His father's disappointment cut deeper than his anger ever could.

THE FOLLOWING AFTERNOON, Edmund was summoned to Dr Carrington's office at the hospital. The senior physician sat behind his desk, fingers steepled, concern etched on his weathered face.

"Edmund, my boy. Sit down."

Edmund complied, already sensing the purpose of this meeting.

"I've known you since you were a lad following your father around the wards," Dr Carrington began. "I've watched you grow into a fine physician. Which is why I must speak plainly."

"About Grace Hartwell," Edmund said.

Dr Carrington nodded gravely. "Word spreads quickly in our circles. Your association with this young woman has raised eyebrows."

"She's a gifted healer."

"Perhaps so. But that's not the issue." Dr Carrington leaned forward. "The medical profession rests on reputation, Edmund. Patients—particularly those who can pay—must trust not only your skills but your judgment. A doctor who makes questionable personal choices faces an uphill battle."

"There's nothing questionable about Grace," Edmund said firmly.

"The world doesn't see it that way." Dr Carrington's voice was gentle but unyielding. "A serious attachment to someone of her background could close doors permanently. Harley Street would never accept you. Hospital appointments would go to others. Even your work at the mission could be jeopardized."

Edmund felt the weight of these words pressing on his chest. Everything he'd worked for, everything he'd dreamed of achieving as a physician—all potentially lost.

"Consider carefully, Edmund," Dr Carrington concluded. "Is this attachment worth sacrificing the good you might do as a respected physician? Worth throwing away years of training and your family's legacy?"

Edmund left the hospital with a heavy heart, torn between the future he'd always envisioned and the one that had begun taking shape since Grace entered his life.

29
JOURNALING

Grace's small room at Mrs Browne's boarding house had transformed with the changing season. A jar of fresh wildflowers brightened the windowsill, and several small pots of herbs—mint, rosemary, and thyme—created a fragrant sanctuary. She'd managed to salvage cuttings from her hidden garden behind the Hartwells' coal shed after being cast out, and now they flourished under her care.

"That's it, Sarah. Now crush the leaves gently," Grace instructed.

Five children sat in a circle on the floor of her room—Sarah, Billy, Tom, and two newcomers, Penny and Alfie. Each held a scrap of paper with dried herbs.

"Will this really stop a cough?" Penny asked, her thin face serious beneath tangled blonde hair.

"It helped Old Maggie through winter," Grace confirmed. "And Mrs Peterson at the market swears by it for her grand-children."

The informal gathering had become a weekly occurrence. What began as Grace simply sharing remedies had expanded to include practical skills—how to mend torn clothing, where to find clean water, which shopkeepers might offer day-old bread.

"Angel Grace," Billy piped up, "can you tell us 'bout your mum again? The one who knew all the healin'?"

Grace smiled, touching the locket at her throat. "My mother Mary could sing so beautifully that people said birds would stop to listen. And she knew every plant that could ease pain or cool a fever."

As she spoke, Grace felt that familiar connection—as if her mother's spirit flowed through her fingers when she worked with herbs or tended to the sick. Each remedy shared, each child taught, each prayer offered wove another thread in the tapestry of her mother's legacy.

"Next week," Grace promised, "I'll show you how to make a poultice for bruises."

After the children left, Grace tidied her room, heart full. Edmund had encouraged these gatherings, even supplying clean bandages and simple medicines from the mission dispensary. His belief in her abilities had kindled something within—a certainty that her worth wasn't measured by the Hartwells' cruel dismissal or society's rigid hierarchies.

"My place isn't determined by where I was born," she whispered to herself, "but by what I choose to do with each day given."

The evening deepened into night. Grace opened her window, letting the early summer breeze caress her face. Stars glittered above London's smoky rooftops, the same stars that had witnessed her father lighting lamps, her mother singing hymns, and her own desperate nights on cold streets.

She pulled her mother's prayer book from its place beneath her pillow. The water damage from that terrible day when Cornelius had thrown her possessions into the street had faded, leaving the pages wrinkled but readable. Grace opened to a blank page at the back and dipped her pen in ink.

I give thanks for this journey, though the path has often been steep and rocky. For the father who taught me to bring light to darkness. For the mother whose healing hands guide mine still. For Edmund, whose kindness showed me I deserve more than mere survival.

I vow to continue healing, to ease suffering where I find it, to create family from the forgotten. The clinic Edmund and I dream of will become real—a place where all are treated with dignity regardless of their purse or position.

With each remedy mixed, each wound bound, each spirit comforted, I honour those who loved me and extend that love outward like ripples in a pond.

Grace paused, pen hovering over the page. Edmund's face filled her thoughts—his bright blue eyes alight with passion when discussing their shared vision, his gentle hands demonstrating how to properly dress a wound, his laughter when she'd correctly identified a complex medical term from his journals.

"Be with him," she whispered into the night. "Guide his path as you've guided mine."

Grace closed the book and held it to her heart. Whatever obstacles lay ahead—the disapproval of Edmund's family, the prejudice of society, her own doubts about deserving such happiness—she would face them with the same determination that had kept her alive on London's unforgiving streets.

"I am Mary's daughter," she affirmed, voice growing stronger. "I am William's child. I am Grace Hartwell, and I will not be defined by others' limitations."

The stars seemed to brighten in response, witnesses to her resolve.

30
A SCALPEL

Edmund stood by the hearth in his father's study, the crackling fire doing nothing to warm the chill between them. Dr Reginald Coulson sat behind his imposing mahogany desk, a fortress of authority separating father from son. The room's polished surfaces and leather-bound medical tomes reflected the elder Coulson's carefully constructed world—orderly, prestigious, and utterly unyielding.

"Edinburgh's Royal Infirmary has agreed to accept you for advanced training," Reginald announced, shuffling papers with deliberate precision. "Dr McAllister is an old colleague. The position begins next month."

Edmund's heart plummeted. "Father, I've made commitments at St Bartholomew's. The dispensary needs—"

"The dispensary will manage without you." Reginald's voice sliced through Edmund's protest. "This is not a request, Edmund. It is what's best for your future."

"My future?" Edmund stepped forward. "Or the future you've designed for me?"

Reginald's eyes narrowed. The fire cast deep shadows

across his face, hardening his features into something almost predatory.

"I've invested everything in your education, your standing in society. I will not watch you throw it away on some ... infatuation with a street girl."

"Grace Hartwell is a gifted healer with knowledge that complements modern medicine. She's intelligent, compassionate—"

"She's a distraction," Reginald snapped, rising from his chair. "One that threatens everything we've built. The Coulson name has meant something in medical circles for two generations. I won't see it dragged through the gutters of Whitechapel."

Edmund flinched at his father's tone but held his ground. "You haven't even met her."

"I don't need to meet her to understand what she represents." Reginald circled the desk, closing the distance between them. "Edinburgh is non-negotiable. Either you go willingly, or you go without my support—financial or otherwise."

The threat hung in the air between them, heavy with implication. Without his father's connections and finances, Edmund's medical career would crumble before it truly began. No respectable hospital would hire him, no practice would accept him as partner.

"Three years in Edinburgh," Reginald continued, his voice softening to something almost reasonable. "Time to focus on your studies, to make connections with the right sort of people. When you return to London, you'll thank me."

Edmund stared into the fire, seeing not flames but Grace's face—her determined green eyes, the gentle way she spoke to patients, how she'd transformed the mission's humble dispensary into a place of true healing.

"And if I refuse?"

Reginald's expression hardened. "Then you are no longer my son. No position, no inheritance, no family name to open doors. Is that what you want? To throw away everything for a girl who can offer you nothing but poverty and disgrace?"

Edmund felt the weight of generations pressing down upon his shoulders. The Coulson legacy, his mother's tearful pleas, the patients who might benefit from his training—all balanced against his feelings for Grace and their shared vision.

"I need time to consider," he managed, his voice tight.

"Consider quickly," Reginald replied, returning to his desk. "The mission board meets tomorrow."

"The mission board? What does that have to do with Edinburgh?"

Reginald didn't look up from his papers. "I've requested they revoke Miss Hartwell's access to the dispensary. Her unqualified interference with medical treatments poses a liability."

"You can't do that!" Edmund's voice rose. "Grace has helped dozens of patients when conventional treatments failed. The mission needs her."

"What the mission needs is proper medical supervision, not folk remedies from a girl with no formal training." Reginald's tone was measured, reasonable—the voice he used to convince difficult patients. "I'm merely expressing concern as a medical professional and benefactor."

"You're punishing her because of me."

"I'm protecting the mission's reputation—and yours." Reginald stood again, straightening his waistcoat. "The board meeting is at ten. I suggest you spend tonight considering your priorities, Edmund. Your future depends on it."

THE FOLLOWING MORNING, Edmund watched helplessly from the back of the mission's meeting room as his father addressed the board. Reginald Coulson cut an impressive figure—his silver-streaked hair and perfectly tailored suit lending gravitas to every word.

"Gentlemen, I speak not as a powerful physician, but as a concerned father," Reginald began, his voice warm with apparent sincerity. "While Miss Hartwell's intentions may be pure, her influence has become problematic."

The board members nodded sympathetically. Most were peers of Reginald's—men who moved in the same social circles, attended the same clubs.

"My son's reputation—indeed, his very future—is at stake. And more importantly, the mission's good work could be compromised by association with unqualified practitioners."

Edmund clenched his fists as his father continued, painting Grace as a well-meaning but dangerous influence. Each reasonable argument, each concerned nod from board members, each sympathetic glance in Edmund's direction felt like another brick in the wall being built between him and Grace.

"I therefore recommend Miss Hartwell's removal from any duties involving patient care," Reginald concluded. "For her own protection, as well as that of the mission."

Edmund knew a decision would not be made final until various regulations had been fulfilled, giving Grace at least a week, but he could feel the board leaning into what his father was saying.

As the board members murmured their agreement, Edmund stared at his father's back, seeing for the first time not the man he'd admired all his life, but a stranger wielding power like a scalpel—precise, calculated, and utterly without mercy.

31
WHISPERS

Grace sat on the edge of her narrow bed, twisting her mother's locket between her fingers. The whispers had reached her first through Ronny, who'd overheard two mission volunteers discussing her fate near the back entrance. Then Miss Peters, a kind-hearted volunteer who'd always slipped Grace extra bandages for the warehouse children, had confirmed it with tearful eyes.

"They're saying you mustn't treat patients anymore, Grace. Dr Coulson's father—the elder Dr Coulson—he's convinced the board you're a liability."

The words hung in Grace's small room like a physical presence. She'd spent the night staring at the ceiling, the moonlight casting shadows that seemed to mock her dreams of a clinic with Edmund.

"A lamplighter's daughter treating the sick?" She whispered to the empty room. "What were you thinking?"

Grace moved to her window, watching London's early risers trudge through the grey morning. Somewhere across the city, Dr Reginald Coulson was likely enjoying his breakfast, untroubled by the life he'd just upended. A man of such power could reshape her world with mere words.

Her hand trembled as she opened her mother's prayer book. The familiar pages offered no comfort tonight. How many times had Edmund praised her healing knowledge? Had it all been misplaced kindness?

"Partners in healing," she murmured, recalling Edmund's words. The memory ached in her chest.

Grace lit her small candle and pulled out her journal, leafing through pages of carefully recorded remedies. Was this knowledge truly dangerous, as Reginald suggested? Or was her real danger the audacity to reach beyond her station—to imagine herself worthy of Edmund's regard?

She thought of the warehouse children who depended on her remedies, the dock workers whose families ate because she'd kept them working despite injuries. What would become of them?

More troubling still was the question of Edmund. Would he fight for her? Could he? Or would he yield to his father's influence, trading their shared vision for the security of his birthright?

Grace closed her eyes, her mother's locket warm against her palm. "What would you do, Mama?" she whispered into the darkness. But no answer came.

32
A MESSAGE

E dmund paced the length of his room, each turn more furious than the last. His father's ultimatum reverberated in his mind—Edinburgh or disownment. The choice that was no choice at all.

The family's Mayfair residence felt like a prison. Its high ceilings and polished furniture—once symbols of achievement —now mocked him with their cold perfection. Edmund ran his fingers through his hair, disheveling what little order remained in his appearance.

He muttered to himself, stopping before the window that overlooked the manicured garden below.

Three years in Edinburgh. Three years away from London, away from St Bartholomew's, away from Grace. His father had orchestrated it perfectly—the board meeting, the concerned speeches, the sympathetic nods from men who'd never set foot in the dispensary. It was a surgical extraction, clean and precise, exactly as his father had taught him to operate.

Edmund's medical bag sat open on his bed, its contents spilling across the counterpane. He'd begun packing it, then stopped, overcome with the absurdity of it all. What good was his training if he couldn't use it to help those who needed it most?

He picked up his stethoscope, remembering Grace's wonder when he'd first shown her how to use it. How she'd listened to his heart with such concentration, her forehead creased in that particular way. What had she heard in those beats? Had she detected the growing affection he'd been too cautious to express?

Edmund crossed to his desk and pulled out a sheet of paper. His hand hovered over it, uncertain. What could he possibly write that would make sense of this? How could he explain that he was leaving when every instinct told him to stay?

The words wouldn't come. Instead, he reached for his coat and hat.

"I'm going out," he announced to his startled valet who had appeared in the doorway.

"But sir, your father has requested—"

"I'm aware of what my father has requested," Edmund replied, his voice clipped. "I'll return before dinner."

The streets of London embraced him with their familiar chaos—a welcome contrast to the stifling order of his family home. Edmund walked without direction at first, letting the city's pulse guide him. Somehow, he found himself near the mission dispensary.

He couldn't go in—not after yesterday's board meeting—but he lingered across the street, watching the flow of patients. How many of them would Grace have helped with her gentle hands and quiet wisdom? How many would now go without care because his father deemed her knowledge dangerous?

A familiar figure darted from an alleyway—Ronny, the

street urchin Grace had befriended. He was now more man than boy, his sharp eyes spotted Edmund immediately.

"Doctor!" Ronny called, approaching with caution. "You ain't inside today?"

"No, not today," Edmund replied, studying the boy's thin face. "How is your cough?"

"Better since Angel Grace gave me that syrup." Ronny kicked at a loose stone. "They saying she can't help at the mission no more. That true?"

Edmund's throat tightened. "I'm afraid so."

"That ain't right," Ronny declared with the straightforward morality of youth. "She helps people."

"Yes, she does." Edmund reached into his pocket and withdrew a coin. "Ronny, would you deliver a message to Grace for me?"

The boy's eyes narrowed with suspicion. "You leaving her too?"

The accusation stung with its accuracy. "I have to go away for a time. It's ... complicated. But I need to see her before I go."

Ronny's expression softened slightly. "She's been crying, y'know. Trying to hide it, but we can tell."

Edmund closed his eyes briefly, the image of Grace's tears like a physical pain. "Tell her to meet me tonight at eight. At the corner of Bell Street and Campton Lane."

"That's where her father used to light the lamps," Ronny noted.

"I know." Edmund pressed the coin into Ronny's palm. "Will you tell her?"

Ronny pocketed the coin. "I'll tell her. But Doctor ..."

"Yes?"

"If you hurt her more, you'll answer to me." Ronny's thin chest puffed out with protective bravado.

Despite everything, Edmund smiled. "I'd expect nothing less."

As Ronny disappeared into the crowd, Edmund continued walking. He found himself tracing the route Grace had described to him—the path her father had walked each evening, bringing light to London's darkening streets.

Tonight, he would meet her there. Not as Dr Coulson, heir to his father's practice, but as Edmund—the man who had discovered his heart's true calling in a mission dispensary beside a remarkable woman.

33
REMEMBER THE DREAM

Bell Street and Campton Lane stood bathed in the soft glow of gaslight, each lamp marking the familiar route that had once been her father's nightly duty. Grace arrived early, her heart fluttering like a trapped bird. She paused beneath the nearest lamp, watching the flame dance behind its glass cage. The light caught the worn cobblestones, casting long shadows that stretched toward her feet like fingers from the past.

Ronny's message had pulled her from the depths of despair. Edmund wanted to see her—here, of all places, where her father had once brought light to London's darkness. She adjusted her shawl against the evening chill, the weight of her mother's locket heavy against her chest.

A figure emerged from the mist, tall and purposeful. Edmund. The sight of him stole her breath. He wore no doctor's coat tonight, just a simple dark suit that made him look both younger and somehow more vulnerable.

"You came," he said, his voice catching slightly.

"Of course I came." Grace stepped forward, close enough to

see the weariness etched around his eyes. "Ronny said it was important."

Edmund's gaze traveled over her face as if memorising every detail. Above them, the lamplighter made his rounds, each newly lit flame casting their shadows in different directions, overlapping and separating with the shifting light.

"My father has arranged for me to complete my training in Edinburgh," Edmund said finally, the words falling between them like stones. "I'm to leave next week."

Grace absorbed the blow silently, though something inside her crumbled. "Edinburgh. That's... that's a fine opportunity."

"It's exile," Edmund corrected, his voice hardening. "A way to separate us."

A hansom cab clattered past, momentarily drowning out the sounds of their breathing. When silence returned, it felt heavier than before.

"How long?" Grace managed to ask.

"Three years."

Three years. The words echoed in her mind, each repetition sharper than the last. Three falls, three winters, three springs, three summers without him. She thought of the clinic they'd planned, the patients they'd hoped to help together. Dreams dissolving like morning mist.

Edmund took her hands in his, his touch sending warmth through her chilled fingers. "Grace, look at me."

She raised her eyes to his, finding them bright with an intensity that made her heart stumble.

"I will come back for you," he promised. "Three years will pass, and I'll return to London—to you. Whatever my father threatens, whatever society dictates, I won't let it stand between us."

The lamplight caught his face, illuminating the determination etched there. Grace wanted desperately to believe him, to cling to his promise like a lifeline. But she'd seen too much of how the world worked, how it crushed beautiful things beneath its heel without remorse.

"Edmund," she said softly, squeezing his hands before gently pulling away. "You mustn't make promises you can't keep."

"Grace—"

"No." She shook her head, summoning strength from some hidden reserve. "Edinburgh will open doors for you. You'll meet people of your own station, form connections that will help your career. Perhaps ... perhaps you'll find someone suitable there."

The words tasted bitter, but she forced them out. Better to release him now than to chain him to a promise that would only bring him pain.

"Is that what you think?" Edmund stepped closer, his voice low and urgent. "That I could simply replace you? That my feelings are so shallow?"

"I think your father is right about one thing," Grace replied, fighting to keep her voice steady. "I would bring complications to your life. Your patients, your colleagues—they would never accept me."

"Then they would be fools," Edmund declared, "and I would have no desire for their acceptance."

A ghost of a smile touched Grace's lips. "The world is full of fools, then."

Edmund reached into his coat and withdrew a leather bag —his medical bag, the one he carried to every house call, every emergency. He pressed it into her hands.

"Take this," he said. "Continue our work while I'm gone."

Grace stared at the bag in disbelief. "Edmund, I can't—"

"You can. You have a gift, Grace. A healing touch that comes from more than just medical training." His eyes held hers, earnest and pleading. "Don't let them take that from you."

She ran her fingers over the worn leather, feeling the weight of the instruments inside—scalpels, forceps, bandages, and vials. Tools of healing that could save lives in her hands.

"The mission would never allow it," she whispered.

"Then don't let them know." Edmund's voice dropped lower. "There are people who need help beyond the mission's walls. People only you can reach."

Grace clutched the bag to her chest, overwhelmed by the trust he placed in her. This was more than a gift—it was a way to continue her mother's legacy, to fulfill the purpose that burned within her.

"I'll use it well," she promised. "Every item, every remedy."

The church bells tolled eight, the sound rolling over the rooftops. Their time was running short.

Edmund stepped forward and drew her into his arms. Grace leaned into him, breathing in his scent of soap and wool and something uniquely him. She committed it to memory, alongside the steady beat of his heart against her cheek and the strength of his arms around her.

"Remember our dream," he murmured against her hair. "The clinic, the patients we'll help together."

"I will," she whispered back, though doubt clouded her heart.

When they finally pulled apart, words seemed inadequate. They stood in silence, eyes locked, the gaslight casting gentle shadows across their faces. Grace tried to memorise every line, every curve, every expression that made him Edmund.

"Goodbye, Grace Hartwell," he said at last.

"Goodbye, Edmund Coulson."

He turned and walked away, his figure gradually fading into the London mist. Grace stood motionless beneath the lamp, the medical bag clutched in her arms, watching until he disappeared completely.

Only then did she allow the tears to fall, silent drops that glistened in the lamplight like tiny stars falling to earth. With each step he had taken, the shadows around her had deepened, the weight of her circumstances pressing down with renewed force.

Back in her small room, Grace placed the medical bag on her bed and opened it reverently. Inside lay the tools of Edmund's trade—and now hers. Beneath them, she found his journal, filled with notes on treatments and observations in his precise handwriting.

"Thank you, Lord, for this gift," she whispered, sinking to her knees beside the bed. "Help me use it wisely. Help me honour my mother's memory and Edmund's faith in me."

She opened the journal, fingers tracing the familiar script. Even separated by miles and circumstance, they would continue their work together through these pages. She would learn from him still, and perhaps, when he returned—if he returned—she would have knowledge to share as well.

"I will not let our dream die," Grace promised the empty room, her voice growing stronger with each word. "Whatever comes, I will carry it forward."

34
KNOWLEDGE

The mission matron's face remained impassive as she blocked the doorway, her arms folded across her starched apron. "I'm sorry, Miss Hartwell, but the board has made its decision. Your services are no longer required."

Grace stood on the steps of St Bartholomew's, the spring sunshine mocking the coldness of her reception. The building that had offered her purpose and belonging now loomed before her like a fortress, its doors barred against her.

"Might I at least collect my herbs?" Grace asked, fighting to keep her voice steady.

"They've been cleared away." The matron's eyes softened momentarily. "The doctors said they were cluttering the dispensary... I'm so sorry."

Grace nodded, swallowing the lump in her throat. She knew well enough that it wasn't about clutter. It was about erasing her presence entirely, as if she'd never brought comfort to the mission's patients, never mixed remedies alongside Edmund, never belonged there at all.

"Very well," Grace said, squaring her shoulders. "Good day to you, Mrs Fletcher."

She turned and walked away with measured steps, refusing to let her shoulders slump until she'd rounded the corner.

Three streets away, she paused in a narrow alley and pressed her forehead against the cool brick wall. "They've won," she whispered, her fingers clutching her mother's locket. "They've taken it all away."

But even as the words left her lips, she knew they weren't true. They couldn't take her knowledge, couldn't erase the skills she'd developed. And they certainly couldn't stop her from helping those who needed her most.

That evening, Grace gathered her small collection of herbs and supplies in Mrs Browne's kitchen. The landlady watched with curious eyes as Grace measured dried chamomile into small paper packets.

"What's all this then, dearie?" Mrs Browne asked, peering over Grace's shoulder.

"Medicine," Grace replied simply. "For those who can't afford doctors."

Mrs Browne's weathered face creased into a smile. "Like little Arthur's cough last month? That tea you made worked a treat."

Grace nodded, carefully folding the paper corners. "Just like that."

"Well then," Mrs Browne said, rolling up her sleeves, "show me how to fold those packets proper. Four hands work faster than two."

The next morning, Grace made her way to the abandoned warehouse where the street children gathered. She found Ronny keeping watch outside, he tensed at her approach until recognition dawned.

"Angel Grace!" he called, his face breaking into a gap-toothed grin. "They said you might not come back."

"Who said that?" Grace asked, adjusting her basket.

"Some fancy folk from the mission. Said we weren't to bother you no more." Ronny shrugged.

Grace studied Ronny as he spoke, noticing changes she'd been too preoccupied to observe before. The scrawny boy she'd once shared crusts with had transformed. Though still lean, his shoulders had broadened considerably, his arms now corded with muscle from honest labour.

"You look well, Ronny," she said, genuinely surprised by the transformation. "Healthier than I've seen you in years."

Ronny straightened, chest puffing with pride. "Got myself proper work at the docks," he announced, his voice deeper than she remembered. "Loading cargo mostly. Hard work, but pays fair."

"The docks?" Grace couldn't hide her concern, knowing the dangers and rough characters that frequented the area.

"Don't you worry about me," he grinned, flexing his arm. "Strong as an ox now, I am. Been saving every penny too." He lowered his voice conspiratorially. "Almost got enough for a place of my own. Just a room, mind you, but it'll be mine. No more sleeping with one eye open."

Grace felt a swell of pride mingled with bittersweet emotion. The boy she'd protected was becoming a man who could stand on his own—perhaps even help protect others.

Ronny motioned to the warehouse. "But Billy's got that cough again, and Sarah's hands are all cracked and bleeding."

Grace followed him inside, where a dozen children greeted her with varying degrees of enthusiasm. Little Billy launched himself at her legs, his thin arms wrapping around her knees.

"I knew you'd come," he said, his voice muffled against her skirts.

Grace knelt and opened her basket, revealing neatly wrapped packets of herbs, salves in small jars, and bandages torn from an old sheet.

"The mission may have closed its doors to me," she said, meeting their eyes one by one, "but I haven't closed my heart to you. We'll find new ways to gather, new places to meet."

She pulled out Edmund's medical journal, its pages filled with his precise handwriting and her own additions in the margins.

"We have knowledge," she continued, "and we have each other. Sometimes that's all the medicine we need."

35
THE MATCH FACTORY

The match factory loomed against the grey sky, its tall smokestacks belching black clouds into the air. Grace stood at the gate, clutching her worn shawl around her shoulders as workers streamed past her, their faces drawn and tired despite the early hour.

"You looking for work, miss?" asked a woman with yellowed fingers and sunken cheeks.

Grace nodded. "Is there any to be had?"

"Always need hands at Bryant and May's," the woman replied, her voice raspy. "Though I wouldn't if I had a choice. But mouths must be fed, mustn't they?"

Inside, the foreman—a stocky man with greying black hair and cold eyes—barely glanced at Grace before assigning her to the dipping room. No questions about experience, no concern for her wellbeing. Just another body to fill the endless rows of workers.

"Name's Bill Polton," he barked. "You'll call me Mr Polton. Six days a week, fourteen hours a day. Late once, your pay's docked. Late twice, you're out. Understand?"

"Yes, Mr Polton," Grace answered, straightening her spine despite the intimidation radiating from him.

The acrid smell hit her first—phosphorus, sharp and chemical, burning her nostrils and making her eyes water. Women and girls stood shoulder to shoulder at long tables, dipping wooden sticks into a yellowish paste with mechanical precision. Their movements were swift, practiced, and utterly without pause.

"You there," Mr Polton shouted at a girl no older than fourteen who'd dropped a match. "That's coming out of your wages!"

The girl trembled but didn't dare stop working to pick up the fallen match.

By midday, Grace's fingers were raw and her back screamed in protest. The constant, repetitive motion of dipping matches into phosphorus paste required a particular deftness she was still developing. Every few minutes, Mr Polton would stride past, his heavy footfalls announcing his approach before his shadow fell across her work.

"Faster, Hartwell!" he'd snap. "We're not paying you to dawdle!"

A woman beside Grace leaned closer as Mr Polton moved away. "Don't mind him," she whispered. "He treats us all like dogs. I'm Martha."

"Grace," she replied, grateful for the kindness in the woman's tired eyes.

"Watch your hands," Martha warned. "The phosphorus gets in through cuts. That's how the jaw-rot starts."

Grace glanced down at her already reddened fingers.

"Phossy jaw, they call it." Martha continued. "Your teeth fall out, then your jaw starts to decay. Seen it happen to half a dozen girls last year alone."

That night, Grace stumbled back to her room at Mrs

Browne's, her entire body aching. She counted out her meagre earnings—barely enough for her rent, with precious little left for food. Still, she set aside three pennies in a small tin box under her bed.

"Education fund," she whispered to herself, a ritual that made the sacrifice meaningful.

She collapsed onto her bed, but sleep eluded her. Her hands throbbed, and her throat felt raw from the phosphorus fumes. Yet behind the physical discomfort lay a deeper determination. Each penny saved brought her one step closer to proper training, to becoming the healer she knew she could be.

After a week at the factory, Grace developed a persistent cough that rattled in her chest. Her fingertips had taken on a yellowish tinge, and she noticed her gums bleeding when she cleaned her teeth. Yet she continued, day after day, setting aside those precious pennies.

"You're looking peaky, dearie," Mrs Browne observed one evening as Grace sat exhausted at the kitchen table.

"Just tired," Grace insisted, though they both knew it was more than that.

"At least eat something proper," the landlady urged, sliding a bowl of stew across the table. "Can't heal others if you're falling apart yourself."

Grace smiled weakly. "Thank you, Mrs Browne."

Later that night, after ensuring her door was locked, Grace pulled Edmund's medical bag from its hiding place beneath a loose floorboard. The leather was still supple, the brass clasps gleaming in the dim gaslight. She opened it reverently, as if unveiling a sacred relic.

Inside lay three medical textbooks, a stethoscope, and various instruments whose purposes she was still learning. Grace opened the largest book—Gray's Anatomy—and traced her fingers over Edmund's neat annotations in the margins.

"The radial artery runs alongside the radius bone," she read aloud, following the illustration with her finger. "Compression here can stop bleeding from hand wounds."

She studied until her candle burned low, absorbing knowledge about circulation, respiration, and the nervous system. Despite her exhaustion, these late-night studies nourished her spirit in ways the factory drained it.

The next morning at the factory, Mr Polton seemed particularly vicious. He paced the dipping room like a predator, finding fault with everyone's work.

"You call this acceptable?" he shouted at a young girl, grabbing her arm and shoving her work into her face. "Each match costs money! Your sloppiness costs me money!"

The girl cowered, tears streaming down her face.

"And you!" He turned to Grace. "Daydreaming again? Perhaps you think you're too good for honest work?"

"No, Mr Polton," Grace replied evenly, continuing her work without looking up.

"Don't get smart with me, girl," he snarled, leaning close enough that she could smell the gin on his breath. "I've broken prouder spirits than yours."

That evening, several workers gathered in a small tearoom near the factory. Grace joined them, listening as they shared complaints and small comforts.

"My Mary's got the shakes now," one woman confided. "Can't hold her spoon steady anymore."

"Thomas lost three teeth last week," another added. "Just fell right out while he was eating."

Martha noticed Grace's expression. "First time hearing the real toll?" she asked gently.

Grace nodded. "I knew it was dangerous, but—"

"We all need the money," Martha finished for her. "But we needn't suffer alone."

As they parted ways, Martha squeezed Grace's hand. "Same time next week? It helps to talk."

Grace walked home with a strange mixture of despair and hope. The factory was slowly poisoning her, just as it was all the others. Yet in that small tearoom, she'd found something precious—solidarity, a shared understanding that transcended their individual suffering.

In her room, Grace counted out her pennies again. The education fund had grown, if painfully slow. She opened Edmund's medical bag once more, this time with renewed purpose.

"Someday," she promised herself, "I'll find a way to help them all."

36
GOSSIP

Grace dragged herself toward the factory gates, each step heavier than the last. The autumn morning bit through her thin shawl, and her lungs burned with every breath of the damp air. Two months at Bryant and May's had left their mark —her fingernails permanently yellowed, her cough a constant companion.

"EDINBURGH PHYSICIAN WEDS SCOTTISH HEIRESS! SOCIETY WEDDING OF THE SEASON!"

THE NEWSBOY's shout cut through the morning fog. Grace froze mid-step, her heart stuttering painfully in her chest.

"READ ALL ABOUT IT! DOC TAKES WEALTHY BRIDE AT EDINBURGH CATHEDRAL!"

. . .

THE WORLD TILTED beneath her feet. Grace clutched at a nearby lamppost—ironically, one her father might have lit in years past—steadying herself as blood rushed from her face.

"Miss? You want a paper?" The freckle-faced boy thrust the broadsheet toward her.

"No, I—" Grace swallowed hard. "Which Doctor?"

"I don't know. They all the same to me." The boy shrugged. "Married some lady with more money than the Queen, they say. Big to-do in Edinburgh."

"Silly girl," she whispered to herself. "What did you expect?"

"What was that miss?" The boy asked.

Martha appeared at her elbow. "Grace? We'll be late."

"Coming," Grace managed, hastily wiping her eyes.

Inside the factory, Grace worked mechanically, dipping match after match with robotic precision. The phosphorus fumes stung less than the pain in her chest. She'd built castles in the air, studying his medical books, saving pennies, nurturing that fragile dream of their clinic together.

Now those dreams lay shattered at her feet, as insubstantial as morning mist. The books beneath her floorboard, his medical bag hidden in her trunk—they were relics of a future that would never come to pass.

"It's just gossip," she told herself fiercely. "You don't know it's true."

But the doubt had taken root, a poisonous vine strangling the tender shoot of hope she'd so carefully tended.

37
PROPOSALS

Months slipped by. Winter yielded to spring, and spring to a sweltering summer. Grace's cough worsened, and the yellowing of her gums spread. The thought of Edmund and his Scottish heiress lingered like a persistent shadow, darkening even her brightest moments.

One evening after her shift, Grace trudged homeward, her thin shawl barely keeping the evening chill at bay. The street lamps flickered to life as she passed—each one a reminder of her father and simpler days.

"Grace! Wait up!"

She turned to find Ronny jogging toward her, no longer the scrawny boy she'd met on the streets. At nineteen, he'd grown tall and broad-shouldered, his face losing its childish softness. The dock work had hardened him, building muscle where once there had been only hunger.

"You're looking well," she said, managing a genuine smile.

"Can't complain." Ronny fell into step beside her. "Got promoted last month. Foreman says I've got a good head for numbers."

"That's wonderful." Grace squeezed his arm, pride warming her voice. "You've worked so hard."

"Got my own place now too. Nothing fancy, mind you. Two rooms above the chandler's on Flint Street."

They walked in companionable silence for several blocks. Grace noticed Ronny's unusual nervousness—he kept clearing his throat, his calloused fingers twisting the cap he held.

"Something on your mind?" she asked.

Ronny stopped abruptly. "Might as well say it straight." He took a deep breath. "I've been thinking, Grace. You're killing yourself in that factory. I see how that cough gets worse every week."

"I'm managing," she protested weakly.

"No, you're not." His voice softened. "I've got a decent wage now. Enough for two."

Grace's heart sank as she realised where this conversation was heading.

"Marry me, Grace." The words tumbled out in a rush. "I know I'm not some fancy doctor with books and learning, but I'd take care of you proper. You could leave that death-trap factory. We could have a real home."

"Ronny, I—"

"Just think on it," he pressed. "We get on well enough. Known each other for years now. It makes sense, don't it?"

Grace looked into his earnest face—this boy-turned-man who'd shared crusts of bread with her in the worst of times, who'd fought off bullies twice his size to protect their little street family. She felt a rush of affection for him, warm and genuine.

But it wasn't love—not the kind that had flared between her and Edmund over medical texts and shared dreams of healing.

"You deserve someone who loves you completely," Grace said gently.

"You could learn to love me." His voice cracked slightly. "I'd be patient."

Grace took his rough hands in hers. "You're one of the best men I know, Ronny. Any woman would be fortunate to be your wife."

"But not you." The hope in his eyes dimmed.

"I can't give you what you deserve." She touched his cheek. "My heart isn't mine to give. Even if he's married another, even if I never see him again—"

"The doctor." Ronny's jaw tightened. "Always him."

"I'm sorry."

Ronny stared at the cobblestones for a long moment. When he looked up, his eyes were clear, though his smile didn't quite reach them.

"Can't fault a man for trying." He settled his cap back on his head. "The offer stands, though. If you change your mind—"

"Thank you." Grace squeezed his hands once more before releasing them. "Your friendship means the world to me."

They resumed walking, the awkwardness between them gradually easing. As they neared her lodgings, Ronny spoke again.

"That doctor was a fool to leave you behind."

Ronny kicked at a loose stone, sending it skittering across the cobblestones. His shoulders had slumped, but there was determination in his stance as he turned back to Grace.

"Listen here," he said, his voice firmer now. "If you won't marry me, that's your choice. But I won't stand by and watch that factory kill you bit by bit."

Grace shook her head. "I appreciate your concern, but—"

"No." Ronny cut her off. "I've made up my mind. I'm giving you half my wages each week."

"I couldn't possibly—"

"You can and you will." His jaw set in that stubborn way she recognised from their days on the streets. "It's enough for you to leave that death trap. Enough to keep a roof over your head without poisoning yourself."

Grace stared at him, speechless. The lamplight caught the hollows beneath his cheekbones, transforming the boy she'd known into a man of surprising gravity.

"Why would you do this?" she finally whispered.

"Because I've seen what you can do." Ronny's voice softened. "Remember little Sarah when she had that fever? Doctor at the parish said she wouldn't last the night. But you sat with her, used your herbs and such. By morning, her fever broke."

Grace remembered. Sarah had been burning up, her small body wracked with chills. The mission doctors had given up, but Grace had prepared a tincture from her mother's recipes.

"And old Tom with his festering leg wound?" Ronny continued. "Everyone said amputation was the only way. But you cleaned it proper, used that bread mould poultice. Saved his leg, you did."

"That was just—"

"It wasn't 'just' anything," Ronny insisted. "It was a gift. Your gift. And you're wasting it dipping those blasted matches."

A hacking cough seized Grace, doubling her over. Ronny steadied her with a gentle hand, his point made more eloquently than words could express.

When she could breathe again, Grace wiped her mouth with her handkerchief, pretending not to notice the flecks of blood that stained the white fabric.

"This world needs healers, Grace," Ronny said quietly. "Not more matches."

Grace looked up at the night sky, where stars struggled to shine through London's perpetual haze. Her mother's face swam in her memory—gentle eyes, hands that always seemed to know exactly where the pain was worst.

"I don't want charity," she said finally.

"It's not charity. It's an investment." Ronny grinned, some of his old mischief returning. "When you're a proper doctor with your own practice, you can pay me back. With interest."

Despite herself, Grace laughed. "And if that never happens?"

"It will." His certainty was absolute. "That fancy doctor saw it in you. I see it too. You were meant to heal people, not make matches that'll burn out in seconds."

Grace fingered the locket at her throat, thinking of her mother's remedies, her father's steadfast service lighting the lamps. Perhaps this was another kind of light she could bring to dark places.

"All right," she said at last. "But only until I can stand on my own."

"That's my Grace." Ronny's smile was genuine now, untouched by the earlier pain of rejection. "Always stubborn as a mule."

"I learned from the best," she retorted, nudging his shoulder with hers. "Truly, Ronny, thank you, from the bottom of my heart."

Ronny smiled. "Don't mention it."

They walked on through the lamp lit streets, two survivors bound by something deeper than romance—a friendship forged in London's harshest corners and tempered by shared suffering into something unbreakable.

38
MARKET DAYS

Grace arranged her small collection of herbs and remedies on the wooden crate that served as her stall. The morning sun cast long shadows across Covent Garden market as vendors called their wares. She had secured this modest corner through Old Maggie's connections—a tiny space between a fruit seller and a woman peddling second-hand clothing.

"Chamomile for restful sleep," Grace called, her voice stronger than it had been in months. "Yarrow for fevers. Rosehip tea for winter coughs."

The transformation had been gradual but undeniable. With Ronny's support, Grace had left Bryant and May's match factory three weeks prior. Her persistent cough had eased, the bleeding gums healing, and colour returned to her cheeks. Each morning, she gathered her carefully prepared remedies—tinctures in tiny bottles, herbs bundled and dried, salves in small pottery jars—and made her way to the market.

A young mother approached, bouncing a fussy infant against her shoulder.

"He ain't slept through the night for a fortnight," the woman confessed, dark circles beneath her eyes. "My neighbour said to ask for Angel Grace."

Grace smiled at the name that had followed her from the streets. "What's troubling the little one?"

"Belly pains. Cries something terrible after feeding."

Grace selected a small bottle of fennel oil. "Two drops in a spoonful of warm water before each feeding. Rub his tummy in gentle circles, like this." She demonstrated the motion on her own palm.

The woman's eyes widened. "How much?"

"Tuppence for the oil."

"That's all? The apothecary wanted six!"

Grace wrapped the bottle in a scrap of clean cloth. "I don't need much. Just enough to buy more supplies."

After the woman left, clutching the remedy like treasure, a dock worker limped to Grace's stall. She recognised him—one of Ronny's workmates with a badly healed ankle break.

"Ronny says you might help with the pain," he muttered, embarrassed. "Can't afford to miss work, but it's fierce agony when the weather turns."

Grace prepared a poultice of comfrey and arnica. "Apply this before sleep, wrap it tight. By morning, the swelling should ease."

Word spread through the market. By midday, Grace had treated a shopkeeper's daughter with persistent headaches, advised a laundress on her rheumatism, and provided willow bark tea to an elderly man with joint pain. Each interaction left her feeling more certain of her path, more connected to her mother's legacy.

"You've quite the following," remarked the fruit seller, offering Grace an apple past its prime but still sweet. "Never seen folk trust a healer so quick."

Grace bit into the apple, savouring its tartness. "They trust because they've no other choice. Most can't afford proper doctors."

"No," the woman corrected, "they trust because you see them. Really see them."

The afternoon brought a steady stream of customers. Grace's coins multiplied—not enough for wealth, but sufficient to replenish her supplies and contribute to her lodgings without depleting Ronny's wages.

As the market day waned, a well-dressed elderly woman approached Grace's stall. Her clothes, though not ostentatious, were of quality fabric, her grey hair neatly pinned beneath a modest bonnet. Most striking was her gentle smile, which reached her eyes in a way that spoke of genuine warmth.

"Might I inquire about your chamomile blend?" the woman asked, examining the small sachets of dried flowers.

"It's mixed with lavender and a touch of lemon balm," Grace explained. "Helps with sleeplessness, especially when worries keep one awake."

"Precisely my difficulty." The woman's blue eyes twinkled. "I'm Mrs Demureson. And you are?"

"Grace Hartwell, ma'am."

"Not 'Angel Grace'? I've heard that name whispered through the market today."

Grace felt her cheeks warm. "A nickname, nothing more."

Mrs Demureson studied Grace with unexpected intensity. "I think not. Nicknames often reveal truths about their bearers."

She selected a sachet of tea and a small jar of salve for arthritic hands. As Grace wrapped them, Mrs Demureson continued observing her.

"Your knowledge of herbs is impressive. Family tradition?"

"My mother," Grace replied, surprised by her willingness to

share. "She knew every plant and its purpose. My father said she could cure anything short of a broken heart."

"And where did you train?"

Grace hesitated. "I didn't, formally. I learned from my mother's recipes, and ..." She nearly mentioned Edmund's medical books but stopped herself.

"Self-taught, then. Most remarkable." Mrs Demureson paid for her purchases, adding an extra penny. When Grace tried to return it, the older woman closed Grace's fingers over the coin. "The extra is for your insight. I've consulted physicians who charged guineas without offering half your wisdom."

Their hands remained connected a moment longer than necessary, and Grace felt an unexpected kinship with this stranger—as though Mrs Demureson saw beyond her worn clothes and market stall to something Grace herself barely recognised.

"Perhaps I'll return next week," Mrs Demureson said, tucking her purchases into her basket. "My headaches might benefit from your expertise."

"I'd be pleased to help," Grace replied, meaning it sincerely.

As Mrs Demureson departed, Grace watched her navigate the crowded market with dignified grace. For the first time in months, she felt truly seen—not as a street girl or a match factory worker, but as a healer worthy of respect.

39
MRS DEMURESON

Grace meticulously arranged her stall, sorting yarrow from comfrey and checking her dwindling supply of willow bark. The market bustled around her, a cacophony of voices haggling over prices and quality. Three weeks had passed since her first encounter with Mrs Demureson, who had returned twice for tea blends and conversation.

Today, the older woman approached with a slight furrow between her brows, her usual composed demeanour strained.

"Miss Hartwell," she greeted, pressing her fingertips to her temple. "I find myself in need of your expertise."

Grace immediately noticed the tension in Mrs Demureson's posture. "You're unwell?"

"Headaches. Persistent, throbbing affairs that begin here —" she touched the base of her skull, "—and spread upward like vines. They've plagued me for weeks now."

Grace gestured to a small stool beside her stall. "Please, sit. When do they worsen? Morning? Evening?"

"Late afternoon, particularly after reading. The pain builds until sleep becomes impossible."

Grace nodded, remembering her father's words about her mother's methods. *Listen first, Mary always said. The body speaks its needs if we've ears to hear.*

"Do bright lights trouble you? Or certain foods?"

Mrs Demureson's eyes widened slightly. "Yes to both. Sunlight can be unbearable, and wine—even a single glass— brings on the worst episodes."

Grace considered this, fingers hovering over her collection of dried herbs. She selected feverfew, known for easing head pain, then added butterbur root. Her mind flicked through Edmund's medical text on circulation as she incorporated dried ginger for blood flow.

"The tension begins in your neck, you said?" Grace asked, grinding the herbs with a small mortar and pestle.

"Indeed. My physician suggested it was merely age and prescribed laudanum, which leaves me foggy and ill."

Grace added lavender and a pinch of valerian. "This isn't about dulling pain but addressing its source. Your body is speaking—tension here," she touched her own neck, "poor circulation, perhaps inflammation."

She wrapped the mixture in brown paper, writing careful instructions. "Steep one teaspoon in hot water for seven minutes precisely. Drink half an hour before your reading, another cup before bed. Apply a warm cloth to your neck while drinking."

Mrs Demureson accepted the package, her blue eyes studying Grace with curiosity. "You've not merely memorised remedies, have you? You understand the why of them."

Grace smiled softly. "My mother taught that healing isn't magic—it's listening to what the body needs."

The next day, Mrs Demureson returned to Grace's stall with a lightness in her step that hadn't been present before. The market was quieter, rain having deterred many customers.

"I approached your remedy with skepticism, I confess," she said, settling onto the stool without invitation. "After so many failed treatments from esteemed physicians ..."

"It didn't help?" Grace asked, disappointment flickering across her face.

"Quite the contrary." Mrs Demureson leaned forward, lowering her voice. "I prepared it exactly as instructed. The aroma alone was soothing—earthy yet sweet. As I sipped, warmth spread through my chest, up my neck. By bedtime, the vice grip on my skull had loosened. This morning, I woke clear-headed for the first time in weeks."

Relief washed over Grace. "I'm pleased to hear it."

"Pleased? Child, you've accomplished what Harley Street's finest could not." Mrs Demureson studied Grace with newfound intensity. "Where did you learn such skills? Your mother, you mentioned?"

"Yes, though she died when I was born. My father passed down her knowledge—he was a lamplighter in Whitechapel."

"A lamplighter's daughter ..." Mrs Demureson murmured, something shifting in her expression. "Yet the fruit seller calls you 'Angel Grace,' and the cooper's boy mentioned you treated his sister's fever when doctors had abandoned hope."

Grace busied herself with her herbs, uncomfortable with the praise. "I only do what anyone might, given the knowledge."

Over the following week, Mrs Demureson became a regular presence at Grace's stall, sometimes purchasing small reme-dies, other times simply observing. Grace noticed the woman speaking with other vendors—the fruit seller who often saved bruised apples for Grace, the baker who knew of her Sunday gatherings with street children, even Old Maggie who credited Grace with easing her winter cough.

On Friday, Mrs Demureson arrived carrying a basket covered with a cloth.

"I've made inquiries about you, Miss Hartwell," she said without preamble. "The stories are remarkable—a young woman who treats dock workers' injuries, teaches orphaned children to read, conducts Sunday services in abandoned buildings."

Grace stiffened. "I meant no harm—"

"Harm? My dear, I'm not here to scold." Mrs Demureson removed the cloth, revealing freshly baked scones and a pot of jam. "I'm here because I recognize something in you—a natural gentility, a moral character that transcends circumstance."

She placed the basket between them. "There are qualities that cannot be purchased or inherited, only cultivated through character. You possess them in abundance."

"You're too kind," Grace murmured, touched by the gesture.

"Not kind—observant." Mrs Demureson's eyes held Grace's steadily. "I believe your gifts deserve nurturing. Perhaps we might speak further about how that could be accomplished?"

40
REFINEMENT

G race returned to her small room, bone-weary after a long day at the market. She set her basket of unsold herbs on the windowsill, where the fading light caught the dried lavender and rosemary. Her mother's prayer book lay open on her bed where she'd left it that morning, its pages worn thin from years of handling.

A knock at her door startled her. Mrs Browne rarely disturbed tenants after supper, and Ronny wasn't due to visit until Sunday.

"Miss Hartwell? Are you within?" Mrs Demureson's refined voice carried through the thin wood.

Grace hastily smoothed her skirt and tucked stray hairs behind her ears. "Just a moment, please."

She opened the door to find Mrs Demureson standing in the narrow hallway, arms laden with books and papers, a determined gleam in her eye.

"I do hope I'm not intruding," Mrs Demureson said, peering past Grace into the modest room. "I've taken the liberty of calling upon you at home."

"Not at all," Grace replied, though her pulse quickened with uncertainty. "Please, come in."

Mrs Demureson swept inside, her silk skirts rustling against the rough floorboards. She surveyed the tiny space—the narrow bed, the small table with its single chair, the shelf of carefully labelled herb jars—with an expression Grace couldn't quite decipher.

"I've brought you something," Mrs Demureson announced, placing her bundle on the table. "Tennyson, Shakespeare, Austen—literature every young woman should know. And these—" she tapped a leather-bound notebook, "are my personal notes on proper etiquette, conversation, and deportment."

Grace stared at the books, their leather bindings finer than anything she'd ever owned. "I don't understand."

"I'm offering to tutor you, my dear. Twice weekly, we shall meet here to refine your speech, expand your knowledge of literature, and polish your manners." Mrs Demureson's tone was matter-of-fact, as though suggesting nothing more remarkable than a walk in the park.

"But why would you do this for me?"

"Because talent without opportunity is a tragedy," Mrs Demureson replied simply. "You possess extraordinary gifts—your healing knowledge, your compassion, your natural intelligence. What you lack are the tools to move beyond your current circumstances."

Grace's fingers trembled as she touched the spine of a book. "I couldn't possibly repay such kindness."

"I'm not seeking repayment. Consider it an investment in potential." Mrs Demureson's eyes softened. "Will you accept?"

"Yes," Grace whispered, then more firmly, "Yes, I would be honoured."

The weeks that followed transformed Grace's evenings into

a whirlwind of learning. Mrs Demureson proved a demanding but patient teacher, correcting Grace's grammar with gentle persistence, demonstrating the proper way to pour tea or address persons of varying ranks.

"No, my dear," Mrs Demureson would say, "one doesn't grip the cup so firmly. A light touch—yes, just so."

Or, "That 'ain't' must be banished from your vocabulary entirely. 'Is not' or 'are not'—never 'ain't'."

Grace absorbed every lesson with fierce determination, practicing her new speech patterns while selling herbs, rehearsing posture while walking to market. At night, she read Shakespeare by candlelight, mouthing the unfamiliar words until they began to feel natural on her tongue.

One Tuesday evening, Grace arrived at her room to find Mrs Demureson already waiting—and she wasn't alone. Two elegantly dressed women sat with her, teacups balanced on saucers that Grace recognised as Mrs Demureson's fine china.

"Ah, Grace, do come in," Mrs Demureson called. "I've brought some friends who expressed interest in your herbal knowledge. Mrs Whitfield suffers terribly from insomnia, and Mrs Blakely's daughter has a persistent cough."

Grace entered cautiously, acutely aware of her market-worn dress and calloused hands. But the women greeted her warmly, and soon she found herself discussing remedies with a confidence that surprised her.

"The valerian must be harvested at precisely the right time," she explained to Mrs Whitfield, "and steeped no longer than seven minutes, or the bitterness overwhelms its soothing properties."

Mrs Blakely nodded approvingly. "You speak with such authority, Miss Hartwell. Where did you study herbalism?"

Grace felt heat rise to her cheeks. "My mother was known

for her remedies," she said carefully. "I learned from her knowledge, passed down through my father."

Mrs Demureson smoothly interjected, "Grace has a remarkable intuitive understanding of medicinal plants."

Similar visits became a regular occurrence. Mrs Demureson would arrive with one or two friends—always different women from her charitable circle—under the pretext of seeking herbal advice. Grace came to recognise these encounters for what they truly were: carefully orchestrated introductions to society.

"You're creating a new history for me," Grace whispered to Mrs Demureson one evening after the others had left.

"Not new, my dear—merely selective. Everyone has aspects of their past they choose not to highlight."

Grace touched her mother's locket. "I'm grateful beyond words, but I fear they'll discover I'm not what they believe."

"What do they believe?" Mrs Demureson asked shrewdly. "That you're intelligent, well-spoken, and gifted in healing? Those things are entirely true."

Grace smiled, though anxiety still fluttered in her chest. Each introduction felt like stepping onto thin ice—exhilarating to be welcomed among such women, terrifying to imagine their reactions should they learn of the warehouse, the match factory, or the cruel Hartwells.

"Remember," Mrs Demureson said, gathering her things to leave, "true refinement comes from within. The rest is merely decoration."

41

A NEW REPUTATION

The cry echoed through the narrow hallway of the tenement building. Grace hurried up the creaking stairs, her basket of herbs clutched tightly against her chest. Mrs Cooper from the ground floor had come running to the market just before closing, panic etched across her weathered face.

"It's Mary Wilson, miss. The baby's coming wrong, and there's no money for a proper doctor."

Grace followed Mrs Cooper into a small, stifling room where Mary Wilson lay writhing on a thin mattress. The woman's face was ghostly pale, her nightdress soaked with sweat. Two other women hovered nearby, wringing their hands.

"She's been like this since morning," whispered one. "Baby won't turn."

Grace set down her basket and rolled up her sleeves. "Boil water," she instructed, her voice calm despite the flutter of nerves in her stomach. "And bring clean linens if you have them."

Kneeling beside the bed, Grace placed gentle hands on

Mary's swollen belly, feeling for the position of the child. The memory of Edmund's journal entries on difficult births surfaced in her mind—his precise descriptions of how to identify a breech presentation.

"The baby's feet are coming first," Grace explained, reaching for her basket. "I need to make a special tincture to help with the pain and strengthen the contractions."

She worked swiftly, mixing black cohosh with motherwort and a touch of valerian to ease Mary's suffering. As the woman sipped the bitter liquid, Grace prepared a poultice of comfrey and yarrow to prevent tearing.

"Now listen carefully, Mary," Grace said, looking directly into the frightened woman's eyes. "When I tell you to push, you must push with all your might. Can you do that for me?"

Mary nodded weakly, clutching Grace's hand.

What followed was three hours of intense labour. Grace guided Mary through each contraction, applying pressure to specific points on her back as she'd learned from Edmund's notes, while using her mother's soothing words to calm the labouring woman. When the baby finally emerged—tiny feet first—Grace worked with steady hands, easing the infant's shoulders and head into the world.

"A girl," Grace announced, clearing the baby's mouth and nose before the little one let out a lusty cry. Relief flooded through her as she placed the newborn on Mary's chest.

"You've saved them both," Mrs Cooper whispered, tears streaming down her face. "The midwife lost the Jennings girl last month in a birth like this."

Word of Mary Wilson's difficult delivery spread rapidly through the neighbouring streets. Within a fortnight, Grace found herself called to three more births, each ending with healthy mothers and babies. Between these urgent summons came a steady stream of parents with ailing children—fevers, coughs, mysterious rashes—all seeking "Angel Grace" and her healing touch.

Grace embraced each case with growing confidence, her basket now permanently stocked with remedies for common complaints. She learned to thread her way through crowded tenements, to calm hysterical mothers, to coax medicine into reluctant children. Each success reinforced her purpose, each grateful family added another thread to the tapestry of her new identity.

"You've quite the following," Mrs Demureson remarked one evening as they shared tea. "Mrs Blakely tells me her cook's sister was saved by your intervention during her confinement."

Grace smiled, though she couldn't help glancing over her shoulder—a habit formed from years of caution. "Not everyone approves. Mrs Finley crossed the street yesterday rather than walk past me at the market."

"Mrs Finley," Mrs Demureson sniffed, "would cross the street to avoid a puddle that might soil her precious boots. Pay her no mind."

"I heard whispers at the Baker's 'Street a girl playing at being a lady doctor.'" Grace's voice caught. "Perhaps they're right. What do I know of proper medicine?"

Mrs Demureson set down her teacup with a decisive clink. "You know more than most. You combine your mother's wisdom with what you've learned from Dr. Coulson's journals. That's a rare gift."

"But my background—"

"Your background has given you strength and insight that no finishing school could provide," Mrs Demureson interrupted firmly. "True gentility comes from character, not birth. Remember that."

Later that evening, Grace stood at her window, watching

the gas lamps flicker to life across London. Each flame reminded her of her father, each pinpoint of light a small victory against darkness. She touched her mother's locket, drawing strength from the connection to her past.

Below, a group of children played in the fading light, their laughter rising up to her window. Grace allowed herself to imagine a different future—one with a proper clinic where no child would be turned away for lack of money, where mothers could birth their babies safely regardless of their station.

And perhaps, someday, Edmund might return to find her transformed—not just surviving, but thriving. The thought warmed her more than she cared to admit.

"One day," she whispered to the London sky, "one day."

42

A MENTOR

One crisp autumn morning, Grace was arranging her herbs when a tall, grey-haired gentleman approached her stall. His clothes, though well-made, showed signs of wear, and his leather medical bag bore scuffs that spoke of years of service.

"Miss Hartwell, I presume?" His voice was warm, his hazel eyes kind beneath bushy brows.

Grace straightened, surprised to be addressed by her surname. "Yes, sir."

"Dr Paul Morrison." He extended a hand which Grace cautiously shook. "I hope you don't mind my intrusion, but I've heard quite remarkable things about 'Angel Grace' and her healing touch."

Grace's cheeks warmed at the nickname. "I only do what I can, Doctor. Nothing remarkable about it."

"Hmm." His eyes crinkled at the corners. "Perhaps we might test that assertion. Would you mind if I observe for a while?"

Before Grace could respond, Mrs Timms arrived with her

youngest, a sickly boy of four with a persistent cough. Grace knelt to the child's level, placing a gentle hand on his forehead.

"Still warm, Thomas?" she asked softly.

The boy nodded, leaning against his mother's skirts.

"And the syrup I gave you yesterday—did it help with the coughing at night?"

"Some," Mrs Timms answered, "but he's still bringing up that thick phlegm, especially in the mornings."

Grace nodded thoughtfully. "Let me listen to his chest." She produced a wooden tube from her basket—a simple version of the stethoscope she'd seen Edmund use. Placing one end against Thomas's thin chest, she listened intently, moving the instrument methodically.

"The congestion is shifting," she murmured, "but slowly. I'll strengthen the expectorant properties in today's mixture."

Dr Morrison watched silently as Grace prepared a new remedy, explaining each ingredient to Mrs Timms as she worked. "Horehound to loosen the phlegm, thyme to fight the infection, a touch of licorice for the taste and to soothe his throat. Three spoonfuls daily, and rub this camphor salve on his chest at night."

After Mrs Timms departed, three more patients arrived in quick succession—an elderly man with joint pain, a young woman with monthly cramps, and a dockworker with an infected cut on his palm. Grace addressed each with the same careful attention, her questions precise, her remedies tailored specifically to their needs.

When the last patient left, Dr Morrison stepped forward again. "Most impressive, Miss Hartwell. Your diagnostic instincts are quite remarkable."

Grace brushed herbs from her apron. "Thank you, but I've had no formal training."

"And yet you correctly identified the beginning stages of

pleurisy in young Thomas, prescribed appropriate treatment, and knew exactly when to schedule a follow-up." He tapped his fingers against his medical bag. "Such skills cannot be taught in medical school—they must be felt."

"My mother was a healer," Grace explained. "I never knew her, but my father shared her knowledge with me."

Dr Morrison nodded thoughtfully. "I've practiced medicine for forty years, Miss Hartwell, and I find myself increasingly convinced that modern medicine too often ignores the wisdom of traditional remedies. Your comfrey poultice for that dock-worker's hand, for instance—far more effective than the carbolic acid most doctors would prescribe."

A genuine smile spread across Grace's face. "You truly think so?"

"Indeed." He hesitated, then continued. "I wonder if you might consider sharing your knowledge of herbal preparations. I have several patients who might benefit from your expertise."

Over the following weeks, Dr Morrison became a regular visitor to Grace's stall. Their conversations ranged from specific cases to broader discussions of healing philosophy. Grace found herself eagerly anticipating his visits, preparing questions about treatments she'd read in Edmund's journals.

"What would you recommend for Mrs Gardner's persistent headaches?" he asked one grey December morning, his breath visible in the cold air. "I've tried every conventional treatment with little success."

Grace considered carefully. "Perhaps feverfew, with butterbur root? I've had good results with similar cases."

Dr Morrison nodded, making notes in a small book. "And the proportions?"

As winter deepened, Grace noticed the doctor's hands growing stiffer. He would massage his knuckles absently during their conversations, occasionally wincing when attempting to demonstrate a procedure.

"Arthritis," he muttered one afternoon, struggling to open his medical bag. "Worse every winter."

Three days later, an urgent knock came at Grace's door. Dr Morrison stood outside, his face grave.

"Miss Hartwell, I require your assistance. Mrs Collins is in labour—twins, I believe, and the first is presenting awkwardly. My hands ..." He held them up, the fingers visibly swollen. "I cannot manage the delicate work alone."

Grace gathered her supplies without hesitation, following Dr Morrison through London's winding streets. In Mrs Collins's small bedroom, she found a woman in advanced labour, her face contorted with pain.

"I'll guide you," Dr Morrison murmured as Grace washed her hands. "Trust your instincts."

For the next two hours, Grace worked under the doctor's quiet instruction, turning the first baby, delivering both infants safely, and stemming a worrying flow of blood.

"You have a natural gift," Dr Morrison told her as they walked back through the pre-dawn streets. "With proper guidance, you could become an exceptional midwife—perhaps more."

Grace clutched her basket tighter, hope blooming in her chest. "Do you truly believe that possible, Doctor? For someone like me?"

"I do, Miss Hartwell." His voice was firm. "And I intend to help you achieve it."

43
NEW BEGINNINGS

Grace stood in her room at Mrs Browne's boarding house, gazing at the modest pile of coins on her bed. After months of careful saving—every penny from the market stall, Ronny's generous contributions, and Dr Morrison's occasional payments for her assistance—she had finally accumulated enough for two months' rent at the apothecary shop on Lavender Lane.

"Are you certain about this move, dear?" Mrs Browne asked from the doorway, her weathered hands clasped at her waist. "You've been safe here."

Grace carefully wrapped the coins in a handkerchief. "It's time, Mrs Browne. The room above Mr Henley's shop has proper windows for growing herbs, and being near his supplies will help my work."

Mrs Browne's eyes glistened. "You've come so far from that half-frozen girl who arrived on my doorstep."

"Thanks to your kindness." Grace embraced the older woman, inhaling the familiar scent of bread and lavender water. "I promise to visit often. Perhaps bring some of my headache remedy?"

"You'd better," Mrs Browne sniffed, patting Grace's back. "That's the only thing that touches my migraines."

The following morning, Grace carried her small trunk to Lavender Lane. The room above the apothecary was twice the size of her previous accommodation, with two large windows overlooking the bustling street. Sunlight streamed across wooden floorboards worn smooth by years of footsteps.

"Previous tenant was a seamstress," Mr Henley explained, a thin man with spectacles perched on his nose. "Left rather suddenly when her brother offered her work in Manchester. Been empty three months now."

Grace ran her fingers along the windowsill, already imagining the herbs she would grow there. "It's perfect, Mr Henley."

"Rent's due first Monday of the month. No gentlemen callers after dark, no excessive noise." He paused, adjusting his spectacles. "Mrs Demureson speaks highly of you. Says you've a gift for healing."

"I try my best."

Mr Henley nodded. "My wife suffered terrible with her lungs before she passed. Perhaps we might discuss some of your remedies sometime?"

Grace smiled. "I'd be honoured."

With her few possessions unpacked, Grace stood in the centre of her new home, savouring the quiet. The room held a small bed, a wooden table with two chairs, a washstand, and —luxury of luxuries—a cast-iron stove in the corner. Through the open windows came the mingled scents of the apothecary below—lavender, rosemary, mint, and dozens of other herbs.

The next day, Grace visited a secondhand clothing shop Mrs Demureson had recommended. With careful selection, she purchased two modestly fashionable dresses, a proper coat, and boots without holes. Standing before the small mirror in her room, Grace hardly recognised herself in the navy blue dress with its crisp white collar.

"You look like a proper lady," Ronny remarked when he visited, carrying a small wooden box. "Almost didn't recognise you."

"Do you approve?" Grace asked, smoothing the fabric.

"Course I do. You were always meant for better than the streets." He presented the box awkwardly. "Got you something. For your new place."

Inside lay six clay pots of various sizes. "For your herbs," Ronny explained. "Made them myself at the pottery near the docks. Owner lets me use the wheel sometimes."

Grace traced the uneven rim of one pot. "They're beautiful, Ronny."

The following week, Grace lined her windowsills with Ronny's pots, filling them with soil from the small garden behind the apothecary. Mr Henley, seeing her interest, offered cuttings from his own herb collection.

"Chamomile for the east-facing window," he advised, "and thyme here where it'll get full sun. The mint needs its own pot —greedy thing will take over otherwise."

Each morning, Grace tended her growing garden, pinching back new growth, rotating the pots for even sunlight, whispering encouragement as the first green shoots appeared. The ritual grounded her, reminding her of early mornings with her father and the stories he'd told of her mother's healing garden.

As her herbs flourished, so did her practice. Women who had previously sought her at the market now climbed the narrow stairs to her room, bringing children with fevers, coughs, and rashes. Grace treated each with the same careful attention, combining her mother's herbal knowledge with the medical techniques she'd learned from Edmund and Dr Morrison.

"My Lily wouldn't stop crying for three nights," Mrs Walters told the other mothers waiting in Grace's small room. "Doctor at the dispensary said it was just teething, nothing to be done. Angel Grace made a clove oil that settled her right down."

The name "Angel Grace" followed her through the narrow streets of her neighbourhood. Market vendors nodded respectfully as she passed. Children ran alongside her, asking for the peppermint drops she often carried in her pockets.

"You've built quite a reputation," Dr Morrison observed one afternoon as they walked back from attending a difficult birth together. "Three mothers at the dispensary yesterday asked if I knew Angel Grace."

Grace blushed. "It's a silly nickname."

"Not at all. Angels are messengers of comfort and healing." He tapped his walking stick thoughtfully against the cobblestones. "You have a gift, Grace. Not just for mixing herbs, but for seeing people—truly seeing them."

"I remember what it was like to be invisible," she replied softly. "When I lived on the streets, people looked through me as if I didn't exist."

Dr Morrison nodded. "That's precisely why you're effective where many doctors fail. You listen to the stories behind the symptoms."

Their walks became a regular occurrence, extending beyond patient visits to philosophical discussions about healing and society. The doctor shared medical journals with Grace, explaining new techniques and theories, while she introduced him to herbal combinations passed down through generations.

"The divide between scientific medicine and traditional

healing is artificial," Dr Morrison declared during one of their discussions in Grace's room. "Both seek the same goal—relief of suffering."

"Yet one is respected and the other dismissed," Grace pointed out, pouring tea into chipped cups.

"Indeed. Just as some lives are valued above others." The doctor's face grew serious. "I've spent forty years watching wealth determine who receives care and who suffers needlessly."

Grace nodded, thinking of the families she treated—hard-working people who could never afford a physician's fees. "If only there were a place where everyone could receive proper care, regardless of their circumstances."

"Perhaps there could be." Dr Morrison studied her over his spectacles. "With the right people dedicated to such a vision."

That night, after her last patient departed, Grace stood at her window, watching the lamplighter move from post to post along Lavender Lane. Each flare of golden light reminded her of her father, bringing illumination to dark places.

"I'm trying to do the same, Father," she whispered, touching the locket at her throat. "In my own way."

The herbs on her windowsill cast long shadows in the lamplight, their leaves reaching toward the glass like hands stretching for connection. Grace touched a sprig of lavender, breathing in its calming scent. From street urchin to respected healer—her journey had been unlikely, yet here she stood.

Tomorrow would bring more mothers with sick children, more opportunities to ease suffering. The dream of something larger—a proper clinic where all would be welcome—seemed distant but no longer impossible. With each life she touched, each pain she eased, Grace moved one step closer to that vision.

44
FORGIVENESS

Grace arranged fresh feverfew and rosemary in her market stall, inhaling their sharp, cleansing scents. The morning had been busy—three children with summer coughs, a dock worker with an infected hand, and Mrs Pemberton seeking relief from her monthly pains. Each patient left with carefully wrapped remedies and instructions delivered in Grace's gentle, assured voice.

"More chamomile tomorrow, I think," she murmured to herself, making a note in her small ledger. The market hummed around her—vendors calling their wares, customers haggling, the clatter of carts on cobblestones. This was her world now, so different from the streets where she'd once sold matches with frozen fingers.

A flicker of movement caught her attention—a pair of figures hovering at the edge of the marketplace. An elderly couple, their clothes worn but once fine, now patched and faded. The woman leaned heavily on the man's arm, her face pinched with discomfort. Something about her thin frame and the severe set of her mouth tugged at Grace's memory.

"Need any help with them herbs, Angel Grace?" called Mr Lynch, the fruit seller whose stall neighboured hers. "Got some lovely plums today, perfect for your preserves."

"Thank you, Mr Lynch," Grace replied, her eyes still drawn to the couple. The woman's face—that downturned mouth, those sharp eyes now clouded with age—stirred something uncomfortable in Grace's chest. A phantom sensation of a hand striking her back, the sound of a bucket being kicked over ...

The realisation struck like a physical blow. Agatha Hartwell. And beside her, stooped and grey, Cornelius. The people who had taken her in after her father's death, treated her like a servant, and cast her out onto the streets when she was seventeen.

Grace's hands trembled as she arranged her herbs, memories flooding back—Agatha's constant criticism, Cornelius's indifference, the attic room with its leaking roof, the day they threw her possessions into the wet street.

The couple shuffled closer, clearly hesitant. Cornelius's once-proud posture had collapsed into a stoop, his shoulders hunched as if expecting a blow. Agatha's face bore the hollowed look of prolonged hunger.

"They're coming this way," whispered Mr Lynch. "Want me to send them off? Don't look right, them two."

"No," Grace managed, her throat tight. "It's fine."

Cornelius approached the stall, his eyes downcast. "Beggin' your pardon, miss," he said, his voice cracked and uncertain—nothing like the sharp commands he'd once barked at Grace. "We're told there's a healer here. Angel Grace, they call her."

"I am she," Grace replied, her voice steadier than she felt.

Agatha raised her eyes, revealing yellowish whites and a vacant stare that showed no recognition. "My husband has a terrible cough," she said, her once-imperious tone now thin and reedy. "And my joints pain me something fierce. We've no money for a proper doctor."

"The apothecary sent us away," Cornelius added, a flush of shame crossing his weathered face. "Said we'd had too many promises and no payment."

Grace's heart hammered against her ribs. These people had made her childhood a misery, had thrown her onto the streets without a second thought. Part of her wanted to send them away with harsh words, to let them taste the cruelty they'd once served her so freely.

But another voice spoke within her—her father's voice, reading from her mother's prayer book: "Blessed are the merciful, for they shall obtain mercy."

She thought of Edmund, who had seen worth in her when she was at her lowest. Of Mrs Demureson, who had recognised potential beneath her rough edges. Of Dr Morrison, who had taught her that healing was a sacred trust, regardless of who sought it.

"Sit down," Grace said, gesturing to the small stool beside her stall. "Let me examine you."

Relief washed over Cornelius's face. "God bless you, miss. They said you were kind."

Grace felt a strange detachment as she checked Cornelius's chest, listening to the wet rattle in his lungs. His skin hung loose on his frame, marked by the yellow tinge of poor nutrition. Agatha's hands were swollen at the joints, her fingers twisted like gnarled tree roots.

"How long have you had this cough?" Grace asked, pressing her palm against Cornelius's back.

"Months now," he admitted. "Gets worse at night. Can't sleep for it."

"And your joints?" Grace turned to Agatha.

"Years," the older woman said bitterly. "Started in my fingers, spread to my knees. Can barely hold a needle now."

Grace moved methodically, her training taking over where her emotions failed her. She prepared a tea of coltsfoot and thyme for Cornelius's lungs, a salve of comfrey and arnica for Agatha's joints. Her hands worked with practiced efficiency while her mind whirled with conflicting emotions.

"Our children have gone," Agatha said suddenly as Grace wrapped the remedies. "Our Violet married a sailor, went to America. Humphrey took work in Manchester. Neither writes."

"Left us when the money ran out," Cornelius added, his voice hollow. "Can't blame them, I suppose. We weren't—" He broke off, coughing harshly.

"We weren't kind parents," Agatha finished, her eyes fixed on her twisted hands. "Too concerned with appearances. Too harsh when they failed us."

Grace paused, the words striking a chord deep within her. She studied their faces—truly looked at them for the first time. Beyond the features she remembered with dread, she saw the marks of suffering, regret, and fear.

"Take this tea twice daily," Grace instructed, handing Cornelius a small packet. "And apply this salve morning and night," she told Agatha. "Come back in a week if you're not improved."

"We can't pay you," Cornelius said, shame evident in his downcast eyes.

"I don't require payment from those who cannot afford it," Grace replied. The words felt strange in her mouth, addressed to these people who had once demanded so much from her while giving so little.

"God bless you, Angel Grace," Agatha murmured, clutching the small package to her chest. "They say you're Heaven-sent to this neighbourhood."

Grace watched as they shuffled away, leaning on each other, two broken people bound together by years of shared mistakes. They had not recognised her—the skinny, frightened girl they had tormented was gone, replaced by a confident healer respected in her community.

As the market closed for the day, Grace sat alone at her stall, turning the encounter over in her mind. The anger she had carried for so long felt different now—not gone, but transformed. Seeing the Hartwells reduced to begging for help had not brought the satisfaction she might once have imagined.

Instead, she felt a curious lightness. By choosing compassion over revenge, she had freed herself from the power they once held over her. Their cruelty had shaped her past, but it would not determine her future.

Grace gathered her herbs and closed her ledger. Tomorrow she would see Dr Morrison about a difficult case, visit Ronny to check his persistent cough, and prepare remedies for three expectant mothers. Her life was full of purpose now, her days spent bringing comfort to others.

As she walked home through the twilight streets, Grace touched the locket at her throat, thinking of her mother's gentle hands healing the sick, her father's steadfast light illuminating dark corners. She had found her own way to continue their legacy, even extending it to those who had once sought to extinguish her spirit.

"I chose mercy," she whispered to the evening air, and felt, for the first time in years, truly free of the past that had haunted her.

45
THE RETURN

Edmund Coulson's boots struck the familiar London cobblestones with a rhythm his heart had not forgotten. Three years in Edinburgh had changed him—his shoulders now broader, his face more weathered, his medical knowledge vastly expanded—yet the city welcomed him as if he'd never left. The familiar smell of coal smoke and Thames water filled his lungs, somehow sweeter than the crisp Scottish air he'd breathed since his abrupt departure.

He paused at the corner of Bell Street and Campton Lane, watching a lamplighter extend his pole to ignite the gas lamp. The golden glow illuminated the street where he had last seen Grace Hartwell, her green eyes shining with unshed tears as she urged him to embrace his future without her.

"Pardon me, sir," the lamplighter said, tipping his cap as he moved past.

Edmund nodded absently, his mind elsewhere. Three years of lectures, surgeries, and advancements had filled his days and nights, yet Grace had remained a constant presence in his thoughts. Her voice echoed in his mind during difficult diagnoses. Her intuitive approach to healing influenced his own methods, earning him recognition among his Edinburgh professors.

His father's letters had grown increasingly approving as Edmund's reputation flourished. The latest correspondence carried news that Dr Pembroke was prepared to offer Edmund a position in his Harley Street practice—the culmination of his father's ambitions for him. The letters never mentioned Grace, as if that chapter had been successfully closed.

Edmund turned toward Mayfair, where his family's townhouse awaited his return. His steps grew heavier as he approached, the weight of expectation pressing down upon his shoulders. He had written to his parents of his arrival date but requested no grand reception. After years away, he craved simplicity, not celebration.

The butler greeted him with dignified warmth. "Welcome home, Dr Coulson. Your parents await you in the drawing room."

The familiar hallway stretched before him, lined with portraits of Coulson ancestors who had built the family's reputation in medicine. Edmund straightened his shoulders and entered the drawing room, where his mother rose immediately to embrace him.

"Edmund, my dear boy," she exclaimed, touching his face as if to confirm his presence. "How distinguished you look! Edinburgh has certainly agreed with you."

His father approached more sedately, extending his hand. "Welcome home, son. Your professors speak highly of your accomplishments."

"Thank you, Father," Edmund replied, the formality between them unchanged by time or distance.

"We have wonderful news," his mother continued, her eyes bright with excitement. "Mr Bashford has agreed to the match!

Millicent is absolutely delighted, and the announcement will appear in The Times next week."

Edmund's heart sank like a stone in still water. Though his father had mentioned negotiations with the Bashford family in his letters, Edmund had not realized matters had progressed so definitively in his absence.

"I see," he managed, his voice steady despite the turmoil within. "That is indeed ... news."

"You'll meet with her tomorrow," his father declared, pouring a celebratory brandy. "She's grown into a charming young woman, and her dowry will provide an excellent foundation for your practice."

Edmund accepted the glass, his mind racing. He had met Millicent Bashford briefly before his departure—a pretty, well-mannered girl from a merchant family eager to secure connections to established professions. She had seemed pleasant enough, if somewhat preoccupied with social standing.

"To your future," his father toasted, raising his glass. "Coulson and Bashford—a most advantageous union."

Edmund drank automatically, the brandy burning a path down his throat. Not "Coulson and Hartwell" as he had once imagined. That dream seemed to belong to another life now, a fantasy concocted by a younger, more idealistic version of himself.

46
BACK TO THE MISSION

The following morning, Edmund made his excuses and slipped away from the house before his parents could arrange an immediate meeting with the Bashfords. His feet carried him toward St Bartholomew's Mission, where he had first met Grace. He needed to know what had become of her before he could face the future his family had arranged.

The mission looked much as he remembered—a solid building amid the poverty of the surrounding streets. Inside, the dispensary bustled with activity, the familiar scent of carbolic acid and herbs bringing a rush of memories.

"Dr Coulson!" Miss Agnes exclaimed, her weathered face breaking into a smile. "We'd heard you'd returned to London. What a pleasure to see you."

"Miss Agnes," Edmund greeted her warmly. "How are things at the mission?"

"Much the same," she replied, gesturing to the crowded waiting area. "Never enough hours in the day, never enough hands to help."

Edmund nodded, then asked the question that had burned

within him for three years. "And Miss Hartwell? Is she still assisting with the dispensary?"

Miss Agnes's smile faded. "Ah, no. The board ... well, they felt her methods were unorthodox. She hasn't been permitted to work here since shortly after your departure."

The news struck Edmund like a physical blow. "I see. And do you know where she is now? How she fares?"

Miss Agnes glanced around before lowering her voice. "Officially, I shouldn't speak of her. But the poor folks still seek her out. They call her 'Angel Grace' in the markets and tenements. She has quite a following, particularly among mothers and children."

"She's still practicing her healing arts, then?" Edmund asked, hope rising in his chest.

"Indeed," Miss Agnes nodded. "Dr Morrison—you remember him, the elderly physician?—he speaks highly of her skills. Says she has an instinct for diagnosis he's rarely seen. Of course, she can't practice officially, but ..."

"But the people who need her find her nonetheless," Edmund finished, a smile tugging at his lips. It was so like Grace to find a way to continue her work despite the obstacles placed before her.

"She's done well for herself, from what I hear," Sister Agnes continued. "Has rooms above an apothecary now. Quite respectable."

Edmund absorbed this information, relief washing through him. Grace had not only survived but thrived in his absence. She had built a life for herself, earned respect in her community, and continued the healing work she was born to do.

"Thank you," Edmund said sincerely. "You've eased my mind considerably."

As he walked back through London's crowded streets,

Edmund felt both lighter and heavier. Grace had moved forward with her life, just as she had urged him to do with his. She had no need of his concern or protection. Perhaps she had even found someone to share her life, someone without the complications he brought.

The thought pierced him unexpectedly. He had no right to feel disappointment. He was practically engaged to Millicent Bashford, after all. His path had been set by his family's expectations and his own ambitions.

Yet as he approached his family's townhouse, Edmund knew with absolute certainty that he could not simply slip back into the life planned for him without at least seeing Grace one more time. He needed to know if the connection they had shared still existed, or if it had been merely a young doctor's infatuation, best left in the past.

He decided, he would seek out "Angel Grace" and discover the truth for himself.

47
A WARNING

Dr Morrison leaned forward in his chair, his face solemn beneath his silver-flecked beard. Grace sat opposite him in the small back room of the apothecary, arranging dried yarrow into neat bundles. The afternoon light filtered through the window, catching dust motes that danced between them.

"You've built something remarkable, Miss Hartwell," he said, his voice low. "Your remedies have saved lives where conventional medicine failed."

"I only do what my mother taught me," Grace replied, though pride warmed her chest at his words.

Dr Morrison's arthritic fingers drummed against his walking stick. "That's precisely what concerns me. You practice without credentials, without society's permission."

Grace's hands stilled. "The poor have no access to proper doctors. They come to me because they've nowhere else to turn."

"I understand that better than most." His eyes, kind but troubled, met hers. "But I've heard whispers in medical circles.

Questions about the 'miracle worker' in the East End. About who she is and by what authority she practices."

A chill ran through Grace despite the warmth of the room. "What sort of whispers?"

"Dr Stalwart mentioned you by name at the Royal College gathering last week. He had a patient, with consumption, —a patient you later treated, who recovered."

Grace remembered the woman—skeletal, coughing blood, given up for dead. "Mrs Collins. She needed proper nutrition and rest as much as medicine."

"Indeed. But Stalwart sees only that you succeeded where he failed." Dr Morrison leaned closer. "I didn't think it would become an issue, but these whispers have grown louder. There are laws against practicing medicine without a license, Grace. Harsh penalties."

The reality of her situation crashed down upon her. All she had built—her reputation, her practice, her independence—could be swept away in an instant.

"What would you have me do? Turn away those who need help?" Her voice cracked slightly. "Send children back to die in their tenements?"

Dr Morrison shook his head. "No. I would never ask that of you. I'm merely warning you to be careful. More discreet. Perhaps work through me more often, as my assistant."

Grace twisted her mother's locket between her fingers. "I understand."

"I don't want to frighten you, my dear. But I've seen good healers ruined by jealous physicians with connections." He placed his weathered hand over hers. "You do God's work here. I simply want to ensure you can continue."

After returning home, Grace stood at her window, watching London's streets darken with evening shadows. Women hurried home with market purchases. Children played in the gutters. A young mother carried a feverish infant, the worry etched clearly on her face even from a distance.

These were her people—the forgotten, the struggling, those existing in the margins. They needed her.

Grace's fingers traced the small collection of herbs growing in pots along her windowsill—feverfew, mint, rosemary, thyme—each one a weapon in her arsenal against suffering. She thought of her little dispensary downstairs, of the remedies she'd prepared that morning, of tomorrow's patients already planning to visit.

She couldn't abandon them. Not even under threat of ruin.

Her father had brought light to London's darkest streets. Her mother had healed with herbs and compassion. Grace would honour their legacy, no matter the risk.

"I'll be more careful," she whispered to herself, resolution hardening within her. "But I will not stop."

48
THERE SHE WAS

The morning dawned grey and oppressive as Edmund made his way through Mayfair's pristine streets. It had been another breakfast with his father's colleagues. His smile remained fixed as he nodded politely at their remarks, though inside he felt hollow.

"You must visit our practice, Dr Coulson," said Sir Henry Blackwood, clapping him on the shoulder. "The finest facilities in the West End. Your father speaks highly of your surgical techniques."

"Most kind," Edmund replied automatically. "I look forward to it."

Later, escaping the suffocating politeness of his father's world, Edmund found himself wandering toward Covent Garden. The market's familiar bustle and noise washed over him—a welcome relief from Mayfair's restrained elegance. Here, at least, people spoke honestly, laughed genuinely, lived openly.

He turned a corner and stopped abruptly.

There she was.

Grace stood behind a small wooden table laden with neatly arranged herbs and bottles. Her hair, that distinctive fiery red, was swept back in a simple but elegant style. She wore a dress of modest blue cotton, far finer than anything she'd owned when they'd worked together, yet still humble compared to the silks and satins of Mayfair.

What struck him most was her manner—confident, poised, articulate as she explained the properties of a dried herb to an elderly customer. No trace remained of the hesitant girl he'd known. This woman moved with quiet authority, her gestures refined, her speech measured and clear.

"Two drops in hot water before bed, Mrs Fletcher. It should ease those night pains considerably."

The woman thanked her profusely, pressing coins into Grace's palm. Grace smiled—that same smile that had once illuminated the darkest corners of St Bartholomew's Mission —and Edmund felt his heart constrict.

He stood frozen, unable to approach yet unable to leave. A gentleman brushed past him, breaking his trance. Edmund stepped forward, then hesitated again.

What could he possibly say after three years? How could he explain his impending engagement, his father's plans, the life mapped out for him that led away from everything they'd once dreamed together?

Grace turned, sensing his presence. Their eyes met across the crowded market.

49
THERE HE WAS

Grace's fingers froze mid-count of Mrs Fletcher's coins. The market's cacophony faded to a distant hum as her eyes locked with Edmund's across the crowded square. Three years dissolved in an instant, that familiar blue gaze reaching across the space between them like a physical touch.

For a suspended moment, she was back at St Bartholomew's, sharing remedies and dreams beneath gaslight. Then reality crashed back—the market stall beneath her fingers, her carefully cultivated new life, and Edmund Coulson, standing tall in his fine coat, looking every inch the successful physician his father had intended.

"Miss? You've given me too much change." Mrs Fletcher's voice broke the spell.

"Forgive me," Grace murmured, correcting the error with trembling hands.

By the time she looked up again, Edmund was approaching her stall. Each step he took seemed to compress her chest further, making it difficult to breathe. The distance between them—once measured in miles and months—now narrowed to mere feet, yet somehow felt vaster than ever.

"Grace." Her name on his lips carried the weight of everything unsaid.

"Dr Coulson." The formality tasted strange. "You've returned to London."

"Two days ago." He shifted his weight, a gesture she remembered from whenever he felt uncomfortable. "You look ... well."

"As do you."

An awkward silence stretched between them, filled with the ghosts of easier conversations.

"I heard you've established quite a reputation," Edmund finally offered. "They speak of 'Angel Grace' at the mission."

Heat crept up her neck. "People are kind. I merely continue what we—what I learned."

A young mother approached the stall with a fussy infant. Grace excused herself, grateful for the interruption as she prepared a mild chamomile tincture for the child's teething pain. Edmund stood aside, watching her work with the same intensity he'd once shown when they'd developed treatments together.

When the customer left, he stepped closer. "Your knowledge has grown."

"As has yours, I imagine. Edinburgh must have been illuminating for you."

"It was ... educational." His gaze dropped to her herbs. "I often thought of how you might have improved their methods with your understanding of traditional remedies."

The compliment warmed her, yet reminded her of their separate paths. "And now you'll establish a practice in Mayfair, I presume?"

Something flickered across his face—discomfort, perhaps regret. "My father has arrangements in mind."

Grace nodded, understanding the weight behind those simple words. Of course there would be arrangements—a proper practice, a suitable marriage, a life befitting Dr Edmund Coulson of the respectable Coulson family.

"I heard you work with Dr Morrison now," Edmund said, changing the subject.

"He's been most kind. His arthritis prevents fine work, so I assist with certain procedures."

"He's fortunate to have you."

Another silence fell, heavier than before. Grace busied herself rearranging bottles that needed no rearranging.

"I still have your medical bag," she admitted quietly. "And the journals. They've been invaluable."

"They were meant for you." His voice softened. "Grace, I—"

"Dr Coulson!" A well-dressed man called from across the market. "Your father expected you at Harley Street an hour ago!"

Edmund's shoulders tensed. "I must go."

"Of course." Grace straightened, summoning the poise Mrs Demureson had taught her. "It was good to see you again."

"Likewise." He hesitated, then added, "I frequent St James's Park on Thursday afternoons. Near the duck pond."

The invitation hung between them, neither acknowledged nor rejected.

"Good day, Dr Coulson." Grace dipped her head slightly.

"Good day, Miss Hartwell."

As Edmund walked away, Grace drew a deep breath, steadying herself against the tide of emotions threatening to overwhelm her. She had built this life—this respectable, meaningful existence—without him. Her worth did not depend on Edmund Coulson or any man.

Yet watching his retreating figure, Grace acknowledged the truth her heart had always known. Some connections transcended time and circumstance, remaining stubbornly alive despite all logic.

She turned back to her herbs, methodically arranging dried lavender into small bundles. Whatever came next, she would face it with the same determination that had carried her from the streets to this market stall. Her mother's healing gift flowed through her veins, her father's steadfast spirit lived in her bones.

If their paths were to cross again—at a duck pond or elsewhere—Grace would meet that moment with courage, whatever joy or heartache it might bring.

50
SCRUTINY

One Wednesday morning, as Grace prepared a poultice for Mrs Tennyson's inflamed joints, she noticed a tall, broad-shouldered man observing her stall from across the market. His expensive coat and polished walking stick marked him as someone from the wealthier districts, yet his expression carried none of the curiosity or desperation that usually brought such people to her.

"That's Dr Stalwart," whispered Mr Henley, appearing beside her with a fresh bundle of feverfew. "Treats half of Mayfair, charges more than most earn in a month."

Grace handed Mrs Tennyson her remedy. "What business would he have here?"

"Nothing good, I'd wager." Mr Henley retreated to his shop as the physician approached.

Dr Stalwart's face tightened as he watched Mrs Tennyson hobble away. "You're the one they call 'Angel Grace'?"

"I'm Grace Hartwell, sir." She straightened, meeting his gaze steadily.

"Are you aware that Mrs Tennyson was my patient until last month? As was Mr Chambers, Mrs Barton, and young Thomas Fleet." His voice carried the precise, cutting edge of a surgeon's blade. "All cases I deemed beyond conventional treatment."

Grace maintained her composure. "I merely offer herbal remedies for those who seek them."

"Remedies?" He picked up a jar of salve, examining it with theatrical disdain. "You're practising medicine without qualifications or license. That's not merely inappropriate—it's illegal."

"I make no claims beyond helping those who come to me, Dr Stalwart."

His nostrils flared. "You undermine the very foundation of medical science with your ... folk remedies and market stall consultations."

"Science and tradition need not oppose each other," Grace replied, thinking of her work with Edmund and Dr Morrison. "Many modern medicines are derived from ancient herbal knowledge."

"Your interference in established medical cases cannot continue." He set the jar down with unnecessary force. "A license denotes competence, Miss Hartwell. Remember that."

As he stalked away, Martha from the match factory pushed through the growing crowd of onlookers. Her face was gaunt, her gums visibly receded—telltale signs of phosphorus poisoning.

"Grace," she gasped, clutching the stall's edge. "It's bad at the factory. Worse than before. Three girls collapsed yesterday. Bill Polton's pushing production, making us work faster with the phosphorus paste."

Grace's heart sank. "How many are affected?"

"Dozens. Management denies anything's wrong, says it's just winter illness." Martha's voice dropped. "Ellen's jaw is rotting. She can barely eat."

Grace immediately began gathering supplies—willow bark for pain, charcoal for poisoning, comfrey for inflammation. "I'll come tonight after the shift ends."

Word spread quickly. By dusk, when Grace arrived at the factory gates, a crowd of workers awaited her. She set up a makeshift clinic in the tearoom across the street, treating one after another as they stumbled in, exhausted from their fourteen-hour shifts.

Grace worked tirelessly, cleaning necrotic gums, preparing poultices for swollen jaws, mixing tinctures to draw out toxins. Her hands moved with practiced efficiency, her voice calm as she instructed patients on continued care.

"This will help with the pain," she explained to Ellen, whose jawbone was visible through deteriorating flesh. "But you must stop working with the phosphorus immediately."

"I can't," Ellen whispered. "My children will starve."

Grace squeezed her hand. "We'll find another way."

For three nights, Grace returned to the tearoom. Workers lined up for her treatments, many improving enough to continue working despite the dangers. Their gratitude manifested in small gifts—a handkerchief, fresh bread, a few precious pennies.

On the fourth night, as Grace treated a young girl's blistered hands, the tearoom door burst open. Dr Stalwart entered, accompanied by a constable.

"There she is," Stalwart announced, pointing accusingly. "Practising medicine without license or qualification, endangering lives with unproven treatments."

The constable looked uncomfortable. "Miss Hartwell, there have been complaints about your activities."

"From whom?" demanded Martha, stepping forward. "Not from us. She's the only one helping while Bryant and May denies we're being poisoned."

"The law is clear," Stalwart insisted. "Medical treatment must be provided by qualified physicians only."

"And where are these physicians when we're dying?" another worker called out. "Too busy with their wealthy patients to bother with factory folk!"

The constable surveyed the room filled with workers supporting Grace. "I'm merely here to issue a warning today. But these activities must cease, or there will be consequences."

After they departed, Grace continued treating patients, though her hands trembled slightly. "I won't abandon you," she promised.

The following morning, her market stall attracted an unprecedented crowd. News of the confrontation had spread, bringing both supporters and the curious. Grace worked steadily, aware of whispers circulating about "the herb girl defying doctors" and "the angel of the match workers."

Mr Henley appeared at her side. "You've become quite the controversial figure," he murmured. "Dr Morrison sent word— Stalwart's speaking against you at the Royal College, claiming you're endangering public health."

Grace's stomach tightened, but she kept her expression serene as she handed a remedy to a waiting mother. "I cannot stop now. These people have nowhere else to turn."

"I know." Mr Henley sighed. "Just be careful. Stalwart has influence in places you cannot reach."

As the day progressed, Grace noticed more well-dressed observers among her usual customers. Some watched with disapproval, others with curiosity. A few approached with their own ailments, drawn by stories of the remarkable "Angel Grace."

Her small stall had become the centre of something larger than herself—a challenge to who could provide healing and who deserved to receive it. As Grace worked, she felt the weight of both opportunity and danger in equal measure, knowing that the path ahead would require all the courage she possessed.

51
WALLS CLOSING IN

Edmund stared into his glass, his reflection fractured by the amber liquid and crystal cuts. Around him, silver clinked against fine china as the Coulson family entertained the Bashfords. The weight of his father's gaze pressed upon him from the head of the table, a constant reminder of their earlier conversation.

"Your entire future hangs in the balance," Reginald had warned that morning, voice low and dangerous in his study.

Now Edmund smiled mechanically as Lady Coulson directed conversation toward wedding preparations. Across from him sat Millicent Bashford, elegant in blue silk, her blonde hair arranged fashionably. She possessed a quiet dignity that Edmund might have appreciated under different circumstances.

"Have you heard about this 'Angel Grace' person?" his mother's friend, suddenly interjected. "Apparently she's treating factory workers with herbs and potions. Dr Stalwart is absolutely livid."

Edmund's fork paused midway to his mouth. The name echoed through him like a bell.

"I read about her in the Chronicle," Millicent said, surprising everyone. "They say she's helped dozens of match girls suffering from phosphorus poisoning."

"Dangerous nonsense," Reginald pronounced. "These untrained women dabbling in medicine cause more harm than good. The College is considering action against her."

Edmund set down his cutlery. "Perhaps the College should consider why workers seek her help rather than qualified physicians."

A glacial silence descended. Reginald's eyes narrowed dangerously.

"I've heard she charges nothing," Millicent continued, seemingly oblivious to the tension. "The article suggested she was once destitute herself, which explains her compassion for the poor."

"Compassion without knowledge is merely sentiment," Reginald countered. "Medicine requires rigorous training, not maternal instinct and folk remedies."

"Yet instinct has value," Millicent replied thoughtfully. "My grandfather always claimed his nursemaid's herbal teas cured more childhood ailments than his physician ever did."

Edmund studied Millicent with newfound interest. Her defence was unexpected, revealing a mind less conventional than her appearance suggested.

"Some of our most effective medicines originated from folk remedies," Edmund added. "Digitalis from foxglove, quinine from cinchona bark."

"Edmund has always harboured romantic notions about medicine," Reginald said dismissively. "A phase from his charity work."

"Is that so?" Mr Bashford asked, his tone cooling perceptibly.

"Ancient history," Reginald waved dismissively. "Edinburgh cured him of such youthful indiscretions. Didn't it, Edmund?"

The challenge hung in the air. Edmund felt the weight of every expectation pressing upon him—his father's legacy, his professional future, the security of the path laid before him.

"I learned a great deal in Edinburgh," Edmund said carefully. "About medicine and about myself."

"Edmund has always had a charitable nature," his mother interjected nervously. "Such a kind heart."

"I admire charitable work," Millicent said, meeting Edmund's gaze directly. "It shows character to look beyond one's privileged circumstances."

"There's charity and then there's impropriety," Reginald countered. "Edmund understands the difference now, don't you, son?"

Edmund felt trapped in the web his father had so carefully woven. Every eye at the table watched him, waiting for his answer—his capitulation.

"I understand many things more clearly now," he said, voice steady despite the storm within. "Including the difference between healing and merely treating illness."

Reginald's jaw tightened. "Perhaps we should discuss the wedding date. I believe early June would be ideal."

"Actually," Millicent said, surprising everyone again, "I've been meaning to suggest autumn instead. The gardens at Bashford Hall are particularly lovely then."

As conversation shifted to wedding plans, Edmund caught Millicent watching him with an expression he couldn't quite decipher—curiosity, perhaps, or something more perceptive.

She offered a small, enigmatic smile before turning to answer his mother's question about flower arrangements.

Edmund felt the walls of his future closing in, brick by brick. His father had made the stakes brutally clear: choose Grace and lose everything—position, reputation, security. Yet sitting amidst the finery of his parents' dining room, nodding at discussions of his impending marriage, he wondered what exactly he would be gaining in exchange for what he'd lose.

52
TORN BETWEEN WORLDS

Grace arranged dried feverfew in neat bundles at her market stall, her fingers working methodically while her mind wandered to thoughts of Edmund. Their brief encounter had stirred emotions she'd fought to bury during their three years apart.

"There you are, my dear."

Mrs Demureson approached, her normally pristine appearance slightly dishevelled. The older woman's hat sat askew, and her gloves showed signs of hasty donning.

"Mrs Demureson, is everything all right?" Grace set down her herbs.

"Perfectly fine." The elderly woman's smile didn't reach her eyes. "Though I must apologise for missing our Tuesday lesson."

Grace noticed three ladies passing nearby, their silk dresses rustling as they huddled together, casting disapproving glances in their direction.

"Did you hear?" one whispered loudly enough to be heard.

"Daisy Demureson has taken up with that herb girl. The one they call 'Angel Grace'."

"How the mighty have fallen," another replied. "She used to be received in the finest drawing rooms."

Mrs Demureson's shoulders stiffened, but she kept her gaze fixed on Grace's herbs.

"These look particularly fresh today," she said, voice unnaturally bright.

"Mrs Demureson," Grace began, her throat tight, "perhaps it would be better if we suspended our lessons for a while."

"Nonsense." The older woman's voice turned sharp. "I've never cared for gossip, and I shan't start now."

"But your friends—"

"Those who judge me for recognising quality of character aren't friends worth keeping." Mrs Demureson's hands trembled slightly as she adjusted her gloves. "Though I must admit, Mrs Wellsley's withdrawal of her invitation to the Midsummer Garden Party was ... unexpected."

Grace's heart sank. Mrs Demureson had mentioned the event for weeks, describing the rare orchids and distinguished guests.

"You've been excluded because of me." The realisation settled like lead in Grace's stomach.

"I've been excluded because Harriet Wellsley is a small-minded woman who values position over principle." Mrs Demureson squared her shoulders. "Now, shall we discuss your progress with Shakespeare's sonnets?"

Before Grace could respond, a commotion erupted nearby. Ronny's voice rose above the market din, tense with anger.

"Say that again to my face!"

Grace hurried toward the sound, Mrs Demureson following. They found Ronny squared off against three young men in worker's clothes, his fists clenched.

"Ronny, what's happening?" Grace asked, stepping between them.

"These gents were sharing their thoughts about 'Angel Grace,'" Ronny spat. "Saying she's getting above herself, thinking she's a proper lady now."

The tallest youth sneered. "People talking about how you're too good for the likes of us now. Got yourself fancy friends and charging for remedies that used to be free."

"I've never charged anyone who couldn't afford it," Grace protested.

"Yet you're living above an apothecary while the rest of us scrape by," another challenged. "Forgotten where you came from, have you?"

"She helps more people than your lot ever will," Ronny growled, stepping forward. "And I'll break the jaw of anyone who says otherwise."

"Ronny, please," Grace gripped his arm. "This isn't helping."

"Listen to your lady friend," the tall youth mocked. "Wouldn't want to dirty those clean hands of hers."

"That's quite enough," Mrs Demureson interjected, her voice carrying surprising authority. "Move along, young men, before I summon a constable."

The youths hesitated, then backed away, muttering threats.

"This isn't finished," one called over his shoulder.

When they'd gone, Grace turned to Ronny. "You can't threaten people on my behalf."

"Someone needs to stand up for you," Ronny insisted, his face flushed. "These aren't the first. People are talking, Grace. Some admire you, but others ..." He trailed off.

"Others resent what they perceive as betrayal," Mrs

Demureson finished softly. "It's the price of rising above one's station, my dear."

Grace looked between them—Mrs Demureson, whose social circle was shrinking because of their association, and Ronny, whose protective instincts threatened to escalate tensions further.

"I never wanted to rise above anything," Grace said quietly. "I only wanted to help."

"The world rarely allows simple intentions," Mrs Demureson replied, patting Grace's hand. "Particularly for women who dare to change their circumstances."

As they returned to the stall, Grace caught sight of a familiar figure watching from across the market—Edmund, his expression troubled as he observed the aftermath of the confrontation. Their eyes met briefly before he turned away, disappearing into the crowd.

Grace wondered if he too felt caught between worlds, belonging fully to neither.

53
A CITY IN CRISIS

The first whispers of cholera reached Grace as she worked at her market stall. Hushed conversations among her customers spoke of sudden illness in Bermondsey, of families losing loved ones overnight. Within days, the whispers grew to shouts of panic as the disease spread through London's poorest districts like wildfire.

Grace read the grim reports in newspapers. Each column detailed mounting deaths, overcrowded hospitals, and the exodus of physicians fleeing to country estates. The Morning Chronicle called it "the worst outbreak in decades," while The Times reported on the "abandonment of the poor by those sworn to heal them."

From her window above Mr Henley's apothecary, Grace watched a funeral procession—the third that day—wind its way down Lavender Lane. A small coffin led the somber parade, followed by hollow-eyed parents.

"They're saying St Thomas's has no more beds," Mr Henley said, joining her at the window. "And half the doctors have left London altogether."

Grace's fingers tightened around her mother's locket. "Where are people going for help?"

"They've set up an emergency hospital in the old textile warehouse on Canning Street. But there aren't enough hands." He glanced at her. "They need people who know how to heal, Grace."

That night, Grace couldn't sleep. Her mother's prayer book lay open on her lap as memories of her father's stories flooded back—how Mary Hartwell had tended to neighbours during the fever outbreak years ago, working until her hands cracked and bled.

What would they do now? The answer came immediately: they would help.

Dawn found Grace packing her satchel with herbs—peppermint for nausea, chamomile for comfort, willow bark for fever. She added clean cloths, tinctures, and Edmund's medical journal, still precious after all these years.

"I'm going to the emergency hospital," she told Mr Henley, who nodded solemnly.

"God go with you, Angel Grace."

The warehouse on Canning Street had transformed overnight. Rows of makeshift beds filled the cavernous space, each occupied by a suffering patient. The air hung heavy with the stench of illness and disinfectant, punctuated by moans and whispered prayers. Harried nurses moved between beds, their faces drawn with exhaustion.

"I've come to help," Grace told a weary-looking woman who appeared to be in charge. "I have experience with herbal remedies and nursing."

The woman—Sister Matthews, she later learned—merely nodded and pointed toward a section where new patients arrived. "We need everyone we can get. Can you assess symptoms?"

"Yes." Grace rolled up her sleeves. "I can."

She worked without pause, moving from patient to patient. A young mother with sunken eyes and blue-tinged lips. A dock worker delirious with fever. Children, so many children, their small bodies wracked with vomiting and diarrhoea.

Grace applied her knowledge instinctively. Peppermint tea to settle stomachs. Cool cloths for fever. Charcoal mixtures to absorb toxins. Between patients, she scribbled notes on symptoms and treatments, adapting her remedies as she observed their effects.

By midday, she'd established a small station where she prepared herbal infusions. Other nurses began bringing patients to her when conventional treatments failed, whispering about "the herb girl's mixtures" bringing relief when nothing else would.

"Try adding ginger root," she told a young nurse struggling to get a child to keep down water. "And a pinch of salt— they're losing too much from their bodies."

The chaos parted momentarily as a new group of volunteers arrived. Grace looked up from grinding herbs and froze. Among them stood Edmund Coulson, his medical bag in hand, speaking intently with Sister Matthews.

Their eyes met across the crowded ward. For a heartbeat, the cacophony around them faded. Edmund's face registered surprise, then something warmer—recognition, respect, and perhaps even joy amidst the grim surroundings.

He made his way to her station, dodging stretchers and nurses.

"Grace." Her name on his lips sounded like a prayer of thanksgiving. "I should have known you'd be here."

"Where else would I be?" She managed a small smile despite her exhaustion.

He glanced at her herbal preparations. "Still combining your mother's wisdom with modern medicine, I see."

"It seems needed now more than ever." She hesitated. "I thought you'd be at your father's practice in Mayfair."

A shadow crossed his face. "Father insisted I stay away from the infected areas. Said it would damage our reputation to be associated with the epidemic."

"Yet here you are."

"Yet here I am." His eyes held hers steadily. "Where I'm needed most."

Without further discussion, they fell into work together, as though the three years of separation had never happened. Edmund examined patients, diagnosing with precision, while Grace prepared remedies tailored to each case. They moved in tandem, exchanging observations in shorthand developed years ago at the mission dispensary.

"The boy in bed fourteen," Edmund murmured as they bent over a young woman with severe dehydration. "His symptoms are different—less vomiting, more fever."

Grace nodded. "I noticed. I've prepared a different infusion for him—elderflower and yarrow."

"Exactly what I was thinking." He smiled briefly. "We still make a good team."

By evening, they had developed a system. Edmund's medical knowledge identified the stage and severity of the disease, while Grace's remedies helped manage symptoms that conventional treatments couldn't touch. Together, they created detailed charts tracking each patient's progress, noting which combinations proved most effective.

"Try this," Grace said, offering a paste of crushed herbs. "Apply it as a poultice over the abdomen. It helps reduce cramping."

Edmund did so without question, his trust in her methods absolute. When the patient's pain visibly eased, he made careful notes. "We should document everything. This could help others."

Word spread quickly through the desperate wards. Patients requested "the doctor and the herb girl," their partnership becoming a beacon of hope amid despair. Their success rate with critical cases drew attention from other volunteers, who began implementing their methods.

On the third day, as Grace prepared fresh infusions, Sister Matthews approached with a well-dressed couple.

"This is Lord and Lady Harrington," she explained quietly. "Their youngest daughter has fallen ill. The physicians they consulted have fled to their country estates."

The nobleman looked at Grace with desperate eyes. "They say you have knowledge of treatments that work when others fail. We'll pay anything—"

"I don't require exuberant payment," Grace interrupted gently. "Only that whatever I can teach you, you share freely with others who need it."

She prepared a kit of remedies, explaining each component carefully. "The illness spreads through contaminated water. Boil everything your family drinks. And add these herbs to strengthen their constitutions."

As they left, clutching her remedies like precious jewels, Edmund joined her.

"That was Lady Harrington," he said quietly. "Her husband sits in Parliament."

Grace shrugged. "They're parents with a sick child. No different from any other."

Edmund's gaze softened. "This is why I—" He stopped abruptly.

"Why you what?" Grace asked, heart quickening despite her exhaustion.

"Why I've always admired your approach to healing," he finished, though something in his eyes suggested different words had nearly escaped. "You see the person, not their position."

More wealthy families came seeking Grace's help as the epidemic raged on. She treated them alongside the poorest dock workers, applying the same care to each. Some left donations for the hospital; others spread word of her skills among their influential circles.

Edmund worked tirelessly beside her, defying his father's repeated demands to return home. Each day strengthened their connection—professional respect deepening into something neither dared name amidst the crisis.

"My father sent another message," Edmund confided late one night as they prepared remedies for the morning shift. "He threatens to disown me if I continue working here." He laughed without humour. "As if that threat still holds power."

Grace's hands stilled. "Your engagement to Miss Bashford—"

"Seems trivial compared to this." He gestured to the ward around them. "Being here, working with you—it's clarified everything for me, Grace."

Before she could respond, urgent calls came from a patient in distress. They rushed to help, the moment suspended between them like a promise waiting to be fulfilled when the crisis passed.

As dawn broke over London, Grace watched Edmund tending to a child whose fever had finally broken. His gentle hands and soft reassurances to the anxious mother revealed everything about the man he'd become. In this place of suffering, amidst the worst of circumstances, Grace found herself falling in love with him all over again—not with memories or dreams, but with the flesh-and-blood man who chose compassion over comfort, service over safety.

And in quiet moments between emergencies, she caught him watching her with the same reverence, as though discovering her anew with each passing day.

54
MILLICENT

Millicent Bashford clutched her handkerchief to her nose as she entered the emergency hospital. The smell of sickness and disinfectant assaulted her senses despite the lavender oil she'd dabbed beneath her nostrils. Sister Matthews guided her through the crowded ward, explaining the various charitable efforts underway.

"We've had remarkable success with certain cases," Sister Matthews said, gesturing toward the far end of the ward. "Dr Coulson and his assistant have developed quite effective treatments."

Millicent's heart quickened at the mention of Edmund. She'd come partly out of genuine charitable concern, but also to observe her fiancé in his element. What she hadn't expected was the tableau that greeted her.

Edmund and a young woman worked in perfect synchrony at a patient's bedside. They moved like dancers in a well-rehearsed performance—he examining the patient while she prepared remedies, their hands occasionally brushing as they exchanged instruments and medicines. No words seemed necessary between them; a glance, a nod, a subtle gesture was sufficient communication.

The woman—Grace Hartwell, Millicent presumed from the whispers she'd heard—had a quiet confidence about her. Her movements were precise, her attention wholly focused on alleviating suffering. There was nothing of the street girl in her manner that Millicent's future mother-in-law had so disparagingly described.

But it was Edmund who truly captured her attention. His face, though drawn with exhaustion, shone with purpose. Millicent had never seen him so alive, so utterly present. The stark contrast with his polite but distant demeanour at their family gatherings struck her forcefully.

"They've been working like this for days," Sister Matthews whispered. "Barely stopping to eat or rest."

Something loosened in Millicent's chest—not jealousy, but relief. A weight she hadn't fully acknowledged began to lift.

When Edmund finally noticed her presence, he approached with surprise.

"Millicent! You shouldn't be here—the risk of contagion—"

"I came to see the work being done," she replied, her voice steadier than she'd expected. "Might we speak privately for a moment?"

In a small antechamber that served as a makeshift office, Millicent removed her gloves and faced the man she was meant to marry in less than three months.

"You work well with her," she said simply.

Edmund's expression shifted, caution replacing surprise. "Miss Hartwell is exceptionally knowledgeable about herbal remedies. We've found that combining our approaches—"

"Edmund," Millicent interrupted gently. "I didn't come to accuse or to spy. I came because I needed to be certain."

"Certain of what?"

She took a deep breath. "That I'm not the only one entering our marriage with my heart elsewhere."

The silence between them stretched taut. Edmund's shoulders slumped slightly, not in defeat but in resignation.

"I've been meaning to speak with you," he began.

"Then let me spare you the difficulty." Millicent twisted her engagement ring—a sapphire surrounded by diamonds, beautiful but never quite right on her finger. "I've fallen in love with someone else. Reverend Thomas Mercer. He leads the children's mission at St Mark's."

Edmund blinked. "The curate with the spectacles? From the Christmas charity committee?"

A blush warmed Millicent's cheeks. "Yes. We've been working closely on several projects. He sees me—truly sees me —not as a suitable match or an advantageous connection, but as myself." She slipped the ring from her finger. "I propose we end our engagement by mutual consent."

"Millicent, I—" Edmund seemed at a loss for words.

"You love her," Millicent stated, nodding toward the ward where Grace continued tending patients. "I've watched you for precisely seven minutes, and it's as plain as day. You've never once looked at me the way you look at her."

Edmund ran a hand through his dishevelled hair. "My father will be furious."

"Mine too," Millicent admitted with a small smile. "But I'd rather face their anger than a lifetime of regret. Wouldn't you?"

The relief that washed over Edmund's face confirmed everything. He took her hand, not to hold her back but in gratitude.

"Thank you," he said quietly. "For your honesty. And your courage."

Millicent placed the ring in his palm, closing his fingers

over it. "Thomas has no fortune, no connections. But when he speaks of faith and service, his whole being lights up. I want that life—one built on passion and purpose, not convenience."

"You deserve nothing less," Edmund said warmly. "And I wish you every happiness."

As Millicent prepared to leave, she paused at the door. "Don't wait too long to tell her, Edmund. Life is fragile—this place proves that daily."

Edmund nodded, a new resolve straightening his shoulders. "I won't. And Millicent? I hope Reverend Mercer recognises how fortunate he is."

She smiled, feeling truly light for the first time in months. "Oh, I intend to make certain he does."

55
RONNY'S FIGHT

The sickroom stank of sweat and sickness. Grace pressed a damp cloth to Ronny's forehead, her hands steady despite the fear clutching at her heart. The cholera had him in its grip, turning his once-robust frame into something withered and weak. His eyes, sunken into his skull, fluttered beneath closed lids.

"How long's he been like this?" Grace asked Charlotte, who'd brought word to the hospital just hours ago.

"Since yesterday morning. Started with the cramps, then the vomiting." Charlotte twisted her apron between work-roughened hands. "He kept saying he was fine, stubborn fool. Wouldn't stop working at the docks till he collapsed."

Grace nodded, recognising the Ronny she'd known since he was a scrappy lad fighting for scraps. The boy she'd protected had grown into a man who protected others, who'd offered half his wages when she needed to leave the match factory.

"I'll need clean water, as much as you can bring," Grace instructed, already opening her medicine bag. "And tell Billy to fetch my larger herb box from above the apothecary."

Charlotte hesitated. "The doctor at the hospital said there's nothing to be done. Said to make him comfortable and—"

"I'm not letting him die." Grace's voice cut through the dim room like a knife. "Not Ronny."

She worked through the night, brewing tisanes of blackberry root and chamomile to combat the diarrhoea, preparing willow bark for the fever. She mixed a paste of slippery elm and marshmallow root to soothe his ravaged digestive tract, spooning tiny amounts between his cracked lips.

When Edmund arrived the next morning, dark circles shadowed his eyes.

"You've not slept," he observed, kneeling beside her at Ronny's bedside.

"Neither have you." Grace wrung out another cloth, the water tinged with cooling peppermint.

Edmund checked Ronny's pulse, his expression grave. "The hospital's lost seventeen more overnight."

"He won't be among them." Grace's jaw set in determination. "I won't allow it."

She'd said the same words years ago when fever had nearly taken Sarah, when Tom's leg had festered after a dockyard accident. This was Ronny—who'd shared his last crust with her, who'd stood guard while she treated the warehouse children, who'd faced down bullies twice his size to protect their makeshift family.

By afternoon, Ronny's breathing grew more laboured. Edmund brought rice water, helping Grace lift Ronny's head to drink. Their hands brushed as they worked, a moment of warmth amid the chill of fear.

"Tell me about him," Edmund said softly as they waited for the next dose of medicine to steep.

Grace's lips curved slightly. "He was the first one who trusted me, after I was cast out. Skinny little thing, all elbows and knees, but fierce as a lion." She adjusted the blanket over Ronny's chest. "He proposed to me once, did you know? Offered to marry me so I could leave the match factory."

Edmund's gaze lingered on her face. "A man of discernment."

"A good friend," Grace corrected. "The best I've known."

That night, the crisis came. Ronny thrashed in delirium, his body fighting the last battle against the disease. Grace held his hand, whispering the same prayers her father had taught her, the ones she'd shared with the warehouse children on cold Sunday mornings.

"Fight, Ronny," she murmured. "You've never given up on anything in your life. Don't start now."

Near dawn, the fever broke. Ronny's breathing eased, his skin cooling beneath Grace's palm. When he finally opened his eyes, recognition flickered in their depths.

"Angel Grace," he croaked, his voice barely audible. "Knew you'd come."

Relief flooded through her, so powerful she nearly swayed with it. "Rest now," she whispered. "You're going to be all right."

Over the next days, Ronny's strength returned gradually. Grace brought broth from Mrs Browne's kitchen, herb tea to restore his vigour, and fresh bread when he could manage solid food.

"You look better than me now," Ronny joked weakly as he sat up for the first time, though his face remained gaunt.

Grace smiled, fatigue etching lines around her eyes. "You gave us quite a fright."

"Us?" Ronny glanced toward the door where Edmund had just entered.

"Dr Coulson helped save your life," Grace said. "We worked together."

Ronny studied them both, something knowing in his gaze. "Always said you were meant for more than the streets, Angel Grace." He reached for her hand, his grip firmer than the day before. "Thank you. For not giving up on me."

"Never," Grace promised, squeezing his fingers. "Not ever."

56
SICKNESS

Grace wiped her brow with the back of her hand, leaving a smudge of something across her forehead. She'd lost track of how many patients she'd treated today. Twenty? Thirty? The faces blurred together in her exhaustion, yet each one mattered. A child with sunken eyes. A dock worker delirious with fever. A mother clutching her infant as both battled the relentless disease.

"You should rest," Edmund said, appearing at her side with a cup of water. "You've been standing for fourteen hours."

Grace accepted the water gratefully but shook her head. "There are still patients waiting. That family from Whitechapel just arrived."

Edmund's concern was etched in the lines around his eyes, but he didn't argue. He understood her too well. Instead, he squeezed her shoulder gently before returning to his own patients.

The emergency hospital had become their world. Days bled into nights, marked only by the changing of shifts and the steady stream of new cases. Grace moved through the wards with determination, mixing herbal preparations that helped where conventional treatments failed. Her feverfew and willow bark tisanes eased suffering. Her elderberry syrups strengthened those recovering.

"Angel Grace," a woman whispered, clutching at her skirts as she passed. "God bless you."

Grace smiled wearily, kneeling beside the woman's cot. "Let's see about getting you some relief, shall we?"

As she worked, a strange heaviness settled in her limbs. She dismissed it as fatigue—natural after weeks of endless labour. The dizziness that followed was harder to ignore, but there were too many needing her help to stop.

"Your hands are shaking," Sister Matthews observed as Grace prepared a tincture.

"Just tired," Grace murmured, though the room had begun to tilt oddly around her.

By evening, her stomach cramped viciously, a pain unlike any exhaustion she'd known. Still, she pressed on, moving from bed to bed until her legs simply refused to carry her further.

"Edmund," she called, her voice unexpectedly faint. He turned from across the ward, his expression shifting instantly from concentration to alarm.

The floor rushed up to meet her. Distantly, she heard the crash of the medicine tray she'd been carrying, felt hands catching her before she struck the floor. Edmund's voice came to her as if through water.

"Grace! Grace, stay with me."

Darkness swallowed her whole.

∼

GRACE DRIFTED THROUGH STRANGE DREAMS. Her father lighting lamps along the Thames. Her mother singing hymns she'd never actually heard. The street children gathered for Sunday services in their warehouse sanctuary. And always, always, Edmund's voice pulling her back when she floated too far away.

"You must fight this, Grace. Please."

Cold cloths on her burning skin. Bitter medicines forced between her lips. The agony of muscles cramping so severely they threatened to snap her bones. She was drowning on dry land, her body surrendering its precious fluids until she was hollow.

"I won't lose you," Edmund's voice again, ragged with exhaustion. "Not now. Not after everything."

Sometimes she surfaced long enough to see him, haggard and unshaven, keeping vigil at her bedside. Once, she thought she saw his father standing in the doorway, his expression unreadable as he watched his son tend to her. But that must have been the fever's fancy.

"Doctor Coulson hasn't left her side in three days," a nurse whispered nearby. "Not even to eat."

"They say he's turned down cases from two lords and a duchess to stay with her."

"His father is beside himself. The match with Miss Bashford—"

"Hush now. Can't you see it's love?"

Grace sank back into darkness.

THROUGH THE HAZE OF FEVER, Grace sensed a presence beside her bed. Not Edmund this time, but smaller, uncertain hands touching her arm.

"Angel Grace?" Billy's voice quavered. "Can you hear me?"

She fought to open her eyes, managing only the slightest flutter of lashes. The effort exhausted her, but she caught a glimpse of several small figures crowded around her bed.

"I brought you this." Something cool and smooth was pressed into her palm. "It's my lucky marble. Found it by St Paul's. It'll make you better."

Another voice, Lizzie's, whispered, "We've been saying prayers for you. Just like you taught us."

"Every night," added Tom. "We even got the others to join. People who never came to the warehouse."

The marble rolled against Grace's fingers as her hand trembled. She wanted to thank them, to tell them she could feel their love surrounding her, but her parched lips wouldn't form the words.

"Stand back, children. Give her air." Old Maggie's familiar voice cut through Grace's confusion. "I've brought something for her throat."

The scent of honey and thyme reached Grace's nostrils. Gentle hands lifted her head, and something warm trickled between her lips. The liquid soothed her raw throat, carrying memories of countless remedies she'd prepared for others.

"That's my girl," Maggie murmured. "Drink it down. You've helped so many. Now let us help you."

"Will she die?" Sarah's frightened voice from the foot of the bed.

"Not our Angel Grace," Ronny answered from somewhere nearby. He sounded weak but determined. "She didn't let me go, and we won't let her go either."

"I promise you, she will it make it through this." Grace heard Edmund say from the corner of the room.

Someone placed a small bunch of flowers on her pillow.

Their sweet fragrance mingled with the medicinal smells of the sickroom.

"We brought these from your window boxes," Lizzie explained. "Mr Henley's been watering them for you."

Grace felt a tear slide down her temple. These children who had nothing had brought her everything—their love, their prayers, their treasures. She'd thought herself alone for so long, but here was her family, gathered around her in her darkest hour.

"Rest now," Maggie said, her weathered hand stroking Grace's forehead.

WHEN SHE NEXT WOKE, the worst had passed. Her body felt impossibly light, as if she might float away without the blankets weighing her down. Edmund slept in a chair pulled close to her bed, his head at an awkward angle that would surely pain him when he woke. His hand rested near hers on the sheets, fingers curled as if he'd been holding onto her.

"Edmund," she whispered, her voice a dry rasp.

He startled awake instantly, disoriented for only a moment before his eyes found hers. The relief that washed over his face was so naked, so unguarded, that Grace felt tears spring to her eyes.

"You're back," he said simply, taking her hand in both of his.

"How long?"

"Five days." His thumbs traced circles on her palm. "The worst case I've seen survive."

Grace tried to sit up but found she hadn't the strength. "The others—Ronny? Old Maggie. Mrs Demureson?"

"All well. Ronny visits daily, though I've only allowed him

brief glimpses of you. You've had a whole troupe of children alongside Old Maggie. And Mrs Demureson sends fresh flowers each morning." He gestured to a small vase of daisies on the bedside table, which sat alongside all the various small trinkets and gifts left by the children. "You truly have done so much for them, Grace. They all love you so much."

"I just did what anyone would have done, tried my best to help." Grace tried to sit up, but found she couldn't.

Edmund smiled, "You have the kindest heart of anyone I know."

"You should have been treating others, not wasting time on me," Grace murmured.

Edmund's expression hardened. "There was nothing more important than keeping you in this world, Grace Hartwell. Nothing."

The fierce certainty in his voice silenced her protests. Something had changed while she'd been lost in fever dreams —something in how he looked at her, how he spoke her name.

"Thank you," she said finally, "for bringing me back."

Edmund smiled, exhaustion momentarily lifting from his features. "Always."

57
SAVING DR COULSON

Grace eased herself from the bed, each movement requiring deliberate concentration. A week had passed since she'd regained consciousness, and though still weak, she insisted on resuming her duties. The hospital corridors bustled with the same desperate energy—nurses hurrying between beds, doctors consulting in hushed tones, and the ever-present moans of the suffering.

"You shouldn't be up," Sister Matthews scolded, appearing at Grace's side with a steadying hand. "Doctor Coulson was quite specific about your rest."

"I've rested enough." Grace straightened her apron, freshly laundered and stiff against her skin. "There's work to be done."

Sister Matthews' expression softened. "Well, at least you've colour in your cheeks again. We thought we'd lost you, Miss Hartwell."

Before Grace could respond, a commotion at the entrance drew their attention. Two men carried in a third between them, his fine woollen coat and polished shoes incongruous among the hospital's usual patients.

"Make way!" one shouted. "It's Doctor Coulson!"

Grace's heart lurched. "Edmund?"

But as they approached, she recognised the grey-streaked hair and patrician features of Reginald Coulson. Edmund's father lay pale and sweating, his normally commanding presence diminished by illness.

"Bring him here," Sister Matthews directed, pointing to a recently vacated bed. "Miss Hartwell, fetch Doctor Edmund at once."

Grace found Edmund in the dispensary, grinding herbs for a fever tincture. His sleeves were rolled to the elbows, revealing forearms corded with tension.

"Edmund," she said quietly. "Your father's been brought in."

The pestle stilled in his hand. "How bad?"

"Early stages, I think. But he's burning with fever."

Edmund set down his tools and wiped his hands. "Where have they put him?"

"East ward. Sister Matthews is with him now."

They walked briskly through the corridors, Edmund's face a careful mask. When they reached Reginald's bedside, the older Coulson's eyes were closed, his breathing laboured.

"Father," Edmund said, reaching for his wrist to check his pulse.

Reginald's eyes fluttered open, unfocused at first, then sharpening with recognition. "Edmund," he rasped. "Didn't want ... to come here."

"Your housekeeper made the right decision," Edmund replied, his professional demeanour firmly in place. "How long have you been feeling ill?"

"Since yesterday. Thought it would pass."

Grace watched as Edmund examined his father with

methodical precision. When he finished, he turned to her with a troubled expression.

"It's progressing quickly," he said quietly. "The symptoms are severe for such early onset."

Grace studied Reginald's flushed face and the telltale signs of dehydration. "I could prepare the willow bark and elderberry tincture. It's helped others with similar presentations."

Edmund nodded. "Please."

As Grace turned to leave, Reginald's voice stopped her. "Not her," he said weakly. "Proper medicine, Edmund."

Edmund's jaw tightened. "Father, Miss Hartwell's remedies have proven effective where conventional treatments have failed. I'll administer them myself if that eases your mind."

Reginald closed his eyes, whether in acquiescence or exhaustion, Grace couldn't tell.

In the dispensary, Grace's hands moved with practiced efficiency, selecting dried willow bark, elderberry, and a pinch of feverfew. As she worked, her mind wandered to the man who'd once dismissed her as unworthy of his son's attention. Now he lay vulnerable, his life possibly in her hands.

"Is that for my father?" Edmund asked, entering the room.

Grace nodded, adding honey to temper the bitterness. "It should help with the fever and ease his discomfort."

"His condition is deteriorating faster than I expected." Edmund's voice was tight with worry. "The hospital is overwhelmed, and even Doctor Morrison is attending three critical cases."

"I'll look after him," Grace said simply.

Edmund's expression softened. "Grace, you're barely recovered yourself."

"I'm well enough." She met his gaze steadily. "Let me do this, Edmund."

Through the night, Grace sat at Reginald's bedside, bathing

his forehead with cool cloths and administering her remedies at regular intervals. His fever raged, and twice she feared they might lose him as his breathing grew shallow and his pulse fluttered beneath her fingertips.

"Fight, Doctor Coulson," she whispered, adjusting the compress. "Your son needs you."

In his delirium, Reginald muttered about patients long past and conversations from decades ago. Once, he grabbed Grace's wrist with surprising strength.

"Rachel?" he asked, eyes unfocused. "Is that you, Rachel?"

"No," Grace said gently. "It's Grace Hartwell."

"The street girl," he mumbled. "Edmund's... mistake."

Grace continued her ministrations without reply. By dawn, his fever had neither broken nor worsened—a precarious balance that could tip either way.

Edmund found her still at his father's side as morning light filtered through the windows. "You should rest," he said, touching her shoulder.

"His fever's holding steady," Grace reported. "I've been giving him the tincture every two hours, and he's kept down a little broth."

Edmund studied his father's face. "That's... remarkable progress, actually."

For three days, Grace maintained her vigil, sleeping only in brief snatches. She prepared fresh remedies, adjusting the proportions as Reginald's symptoms evolved. On the fourth morning, she was spooning broth between his cracked lips when his eyes opened, clear and alert for the first time.

"Miss Hartwell," he said, his voice weak but lucid.

"Doctor Coulson," she acknowledged. "You're improving."

He studied her face with new awareness. "You've been caring for me."

"Yes."

"Why?"

Grace considered the question. "Because you needed care," she said simply. "And because you're Edmund's father."

Reginald's gaze remained fixed on her, something unreadable passing across his features. "I was wrong about you," he said finally.

Grace set down the spoon, surprised by his words. "You should rest now," she said. "Your body is still healing."

As she turned to leave, his hand caught her wrist—not in delirium this time, but with purpose.

"Thank you," he said, the words clearly difficult for him. "For my life."

58
RECOGNITION

G race stood at the back of St George's Hall, still slightly
pale from her recovery, but determined to attend the
community gathering. The epidemic had finally begun to
wane, leaving exhausted survivors to count their losses and
blessings alike. She tugged at her collar, uncomfortable with
the attention her presence drew—whispers of "Angel Grace"
followed her like shadows.

"You should be seated," Edmund murmured, appearing at
her side. "You're not fully recovered."

"I've spent enough time resting," Grace replied, though she
leaned slightly against the wall for support. "I needed to see
this—all these people alive and healing."

The hall buzzed with conversation as families reunited
with loved ones who had survived, while others sought
comfort in shared grief. At the front, several physicians gathered, including Dr Morrison and, surprisingly, Dr Reginald
Coulson, who had insisted on attending despite his own recent
brush with death.

Dr Morrison tapped a glass for attention, and the room gradually quieted.

"Friends and neighbours," he began, his voice carrying across the hall, "we gather today to mark the turning of this terrible tide. The cholera has taken too many from us, but through collective effort, we have weathered the worst."

Grace listened as he acknowledged the physicians, nurses, and volunteers who had worked tirelessly at the emergency hospital. Her thoughts drifted to those they couldn't save—the children who had slipped away despite their best efforts, the mothers who had sacrificed their last strength for their families.

"However," Dr Morrison continued, drawing Grace's attention back, "I must speak specifically about one contribution that proved invaluable. Many of you have benefited from the herbal remedies developed by Miss Grace Hartwell."

A murmur rippled through the crowd as heads turned, searching for her. Grace felt heat rise in her cheeks.

"When conventional treatments failed, Miss Hartwell's combinations of willow bark, elderberry, and other herbs provided relief where we could offer none. Her tinctures reduced fevers and eased symptoms, giving patients the strength to fight. I can state with certainty that without her knowledge, many more would have perished."

Grace's heart hammered against her ribs. She had never sought recognition—had, in fact, spent years hiding her work for fear of prosecution. Now Dr Morrison spoke of her remedies as if they were legitimate medicine.

"Miss Hartwell represents the finest tradition of healing—compassion paired with knowledge, regardless of formal training. Her contributions reminds us that true medicine lies not in credentials alone, but in the heart's determination to ease suffering."

Tears pricked at Grace's eyes. She thought of her mother, whose remedies had formed the foundation of her knowledge, and her father, whose stories had kept that legacy alive. They would have been proud to see this moment—their daughter continuing their work of bringing light to dark places.

After the gathering dispersed, Grace found herself surrounded by well-wishers—mothers whose children she had treated, workers who had recovered under her care. Their gratitude overwhelmed her, each story a testament to the difference her remedies had made.

"Miss Hartwell," Dr Morrison called, approaching with Dr Coulson and several other physicians. "A moment, if you please."

Grace excused herself from the crowd, suddenly apprehensive. Despite Dr Morrison's public praise, she remained acutely aware of her precarious position—still practicing without formal qualification.

"I've been discussing your future with my colleagues," Dr Morrison said, his eyes twinkling with barely contained excitement.

"My future?" Grace echoed.

"Indeed. Given your extraordinary service during this crisis, I've proposed that you be granted special recognition—a formal acknowledgment of your skills that would open doors previously closed to you."

Grace's breath caught. "What sort of recognition?"

"An opportunity for formal training as a nurse-midwife," Dr. Morrison explained. "Under my sponsorship, with recommendations from several physicians who witnessed your work during the epidemic."

"That's—" Grace struggled to find words. "That's not possible. I have no formal education, no qualifications."

"Which makes your natural ability all the more remarkable," Dr Morrison countered. "The Royal College has provisions for exceptional cases. Yours would certainly qualify."

From behind Dr Morrison stepped Dr Stalwart, his face set in disapproval. "This is highly irregular," he interjected. "The girl has no background, no training. We cannot simply waive standards because she mixed a few herbs during a crisis."

"A few herbs that saved lives when your treatments failed," Dr Morrison replied sharply.

"Anecdotal evidence at best," Dr Stalwart scoffed. "Where are her case notes? Her documented results? This would make a mockery of our profession."

Grace felt her hopes crumbling as quickly as they had formed. Of course it had been too much to expect—someone like her being formally recognised by the medical establishment.

"I believe I can address those concerns," came a steady voice. Dr Reginald Coulson stepped forward, still bearing the pallor of his illness but standing straight-backed and dignified.

"Dr Coulson," Stalwart acknowledged with surprise. "Surely you of all people understand the importance of maintaining standards."

"I understand the importance of recognising excellence," Reginald replied. "Miss Hartwell saved my life with her remedies when conventional treatments had failed. I have personally witnessed her diagnostic skills, her understanding of human physiology, and her instinctive grasp of dosage and contraindications."

Grace stared at Edmund's father in astonishment. This was the man who had once orchestrated her removal from St Bartholomew's, who had sent his son to Edinburgh to separate them.

"Furthermore," Reginald continued, "I have reviewed the records from the emergency hospital. The mortality rate among patients treated with Miss Hartwell's protocols was significantly lower than the average. Those are not anecdotes, Dr Stalwart. Those are facts."

Dr Stalwart's mouth opened and closed, his objections faltering in the face of Reginald Coulson's support.

"I will personally endorse Miss Hartwell's application for formal training," Reginald concluded. "And I suspect many of my colleagues will do the same."

Grace felt the ground shift beneath her feet. The possibility of formal recognition—of training that would legitimise her work—was suddenly, improbably real.

"Miss Hartwell?" Dr Morrison prompted gently. "What do you say?"

A thousand emotions coursed through her—gratitude, excitement, disbelief. But beneath them ran a current of doubt. Could someone like her truly belong in that world? Would she ever be more than a curiosity, a street girl playing at being a proper nurse?

"I—I don't know what to say," she managed. "It's more than I ever dared hope for."

"It's no more than you've earned," Dr Morrison assured her, squeezing her hand. "Think on it. We can discuss the details when you've had time to consider."

As the physicians moved away, Grace remained rooted to the spot, overwhelmed by the possibilities suddenly stretching before her. From the corner of her eye, she caught Edmund watching her, his expression a mixture of pride and something deeper, more personal.

"Did you know about this?" she asked when he approached.

"Not until today," he admitted. "Though I'd hoped something might come of your work during the epidemic." He hesitated, then added, "You deserve this, Grace. You've always deserved recognition for your gifts."

Grace shook her head slowly. "I'm not sure I do. There are so many who helped—Ronny, Mrs Demureson, the street children who carried messages and fetched supplies."

"And you acknowledge them all," Edmund said softly. "That's part of what makes you extraordinary."

59
HONOURED LEGACY

The following days brought a strange new reality. Grace walked through streets she'd once navigated as an invisible creature, now meeting nods of recognition, small bows, and grateful smiles. Market vendors pressed apples into her hands, refusing payment. A carriage driver tipped his hat as she passed.

"There she goes—Angel Grace," a woman whispered to her companion, not bothering to lower her voice. "She saved my sister's youngest when the fever took hold."

Grace quickened her pace, cheeks burning. Such attention felt foreign, almost uncomfortable. Yet beneath her embarrassment flowed an undercurrent of quiet joy. Not for the recognition itself, but for what it represented—lives touched, suffering eased, her mother's legacy honoured.

Outside Mr Henley's apothecary, Grace found a small gathering of street children, including several from her old warehouse congregation. They'd arranged wildflowers in a chipped teacup—yarrow, lavender, and chamomile, the very herbs she'd taught them to identify.

"For you, Miss Grace," said little Sarah, now taller and healthier than when Grace had first met her. "Ronny told us you're to be a proper nurse now. With papers and everything."

"Not quite yet," Grace smiled, kneeling to accept their gift. "There's much to learn first."

"But you already know everything about healing," Billy insisted, his once-hollow cheeks now rounded with health.

"Knowledge is a journey, not a destination," Grace replied, echoing words her father had once shared. "There's always more to discover."

Later, in her room above the apothecary, Grace sat at her small table, spreading out the papers Dr Morrison had provided. The nurse-midwife training program would be rigorous—anatomy, physiology, surgical principles, childbed fever prevention. Her herbal knowledge would be only one thread in a complex tapestry of medical understanding.

The enormity of it might have overwhelmed her once. But now, Grace felt strangely calm, even eager. The path ahead was difficult but clear. She would bring her unique perspective to this formal training, combining traditional wisdom with modern medicine—just as she and Edmund had done during the epidemic.

Grace opened her mother's prayer book, now carefully restored after its soaking years ago. Between its pages, she'd pressed a sprig of yarrow—the first herb her father had taught her to recognise. A symbol of healing, of continuity, of light in darkness.

"I'm ready," she whispered to the empty room, her voice steady with newfound certainty.

60

BY LAMPLIGHT

The evening air carried a gentle chill as Edmund led Grace through familiar streets. They walked arm in arm, their footsteps echoing against worn cobblestones. Grace pulled her shawl closer, not from cold, but from a sense of anticipation she couldn't quite name.

"Where are we going?" she asked, noting they had turned away from their usual path.

Edmund's smile held a secret. "Somewhere special."

As they rounded the corner near the Thames, recognition dawned on Grace. This place—this very corner—was where her father had lit the lamps each evening. How many times had she stood beside him, watching with childish wonder as he had brought light to London's darkness?

The lamplighter was making his rounds now, moving from post to post with practiced efficiency. The familiar sight caught in Grace's throat—the long pole extending upward, the quick movement to ignite the gas, the soft whoosh as flame caught and spread. One by one, the lamps flickered to life, casting pools of golden light that pushed back against the encroaching night.

"You remembered," Grace whispered, turning to Edmund.

"Of course." His voice was soft. "You once told me this was where you felt closest to him."

They stood in companionable silence as the lamplighter finished his work and moved on, leaving them alone beneath the gentle glow. The Thames flowed quietly nearby, no longer the threatening presence that had claimed her father, but a steady companion to their city.

Edmund took both her hands in his. "Grace, do you know what I thought the first time I saw you?"

She shook her head, remembering their first meeting—her, half-frozen on the mission steps, clutching her mother's prayer book.

"I thought you were the bravest person I'd ever met." His thumbs traced circles on her palms. "Not just for surviving, but for how you cared for others even when you had nothing yourself."

The gaslight caught the angles of his face, highlighting the earnestness in his expression. Edmund had changed in the years she'd known him—grown more confident, more certain of his path. Yet the essential kindness that had first drawn her to him remained unchanged.

"Every lamp your father lit brought comfort to someone in darkness," Edmund continued. "And you, Grace—you've been that light for so many. For the children at the warehouse, for the workers at the factory." His voice softened. "For me."

Before Grace could respond, Edmund lowered himself to one knee. The gesture was so unexpected that her breath caught. Around them, London continued its evening bustle—carriage wheels on cobblestones, distant voices, the lap of water against the embankment—but here, in their small circle of lamplight, time seemed suspended.

"You have been the light in my darkness, Grace Hartwell," Edmund said, looking up at her with eyes full of certainty. "Just as your father brought warmth to these streets with every lamp he lit. I've known since that first day at St. Bartholomew's that my life would never be the same because of you."

Grace's heart fluttered wildly as tears gathered in her eyes. The memories flooded back—her father's stories, her mother's prayer book, the cruel years with the Hartwells, the warehouse sanctuary, the epidemic that had nearly claimed them both. Every step, every struggle had led her here, to this moment, to this man who saw her completely.

"I love you—your compassion, your courage, your healing hands." Edmund's voice remained steady though his eyes shimmered with emotion. "Will you marry me, Grace? Will you build our dream together—the clinic, our home, our life?"

The lamplight danced around them, casting their shadows long against the pavement. In its gentle glow, Grace saw not just Edmund, but the path that stretched before them—challenging, purposeful, shared.

"Yes," she whispered, then louder with certainty, "Yes, Edmund."

He rose to his feet, slipping a simple gold band onto her finger before drawing her close. Their embrace felt like coming home after a long journey. Above them, the gas lamp flickered and steadied, a beacon in the growing darkness.

The corner where William Hartwell had once brought light to London now held new meaning—a beginning rather than an end, a promise of light to come rather than light remembered. As Edmund's lips met hers, Grace felt her father's presence like a blessing, a circle completed.

61

COMFORT

Grace stood looking over her herb garden, breathing in the fragrance of lavender and rosemary that stretched toward the morning sun. The small plot behind Mr Henley's apothecary had transformed under her care—once barren soil now burst with healing plants, much as her own life had blossomed from its humble beginnings. What had started as a few handfuls of herbs growing on her windowsill, had now become this.

She brushed her fingers across the feverfew, its white petals like tiny stars against the green. The engagement ring on her finger caught the light, still unfamiliar but wonderfully right. Wedding plans moved forward with Mrs Demureson's enthusiastic assistance, and tomorrow she would begin her formal training as a nurse-midwife under Dr Morrison's guidance.

"My cup runneth over," Grace whispered, recalling the psalm from her mother's prayer book.

From the lamplighter's daughter to street waif to healer— each step of her journey had shaped her, hardened her resolve, taught her to find light in darkness. Even the cruel years with the Hartwells and the bitter cold of homelessness had given her understanding that no university could teach.

Grace knelt to harvest some chamomile, filling her basket methodically. Her trained hands moved with purpose, selecting only the perfect blooms. These same hands had once begged for pennies, dipped matches in poisonous phosphorus, and later saved lives during London's darkest hours.

The clinic she and Edmund envisioned would one day become reality. A place where healing knowledge from all sources would be respected, where both wealthy merchants and dock workers' children would receive equal care. She smiled, thinking of Edmund's passionate descriptions of their future practice during their evening walks.

"Grace?" Mr Henley called from the shop door. "There's a woman here asking for your yarrow tincture. Says her baby's teething something fierce."

Grace rose, brushing soil from her skirt. "Coming," she called back, gathering her basket.

Some things would never change—her desire to heal, to comfort, and to bring light where there was darkness. With Edmund beside her, that flame would only burn brighter.

62
BLESSINGS

G race entered the apothecary, where the familiar scent of dried herbs and tinctures mingled with polished wood. Mr Henley stood beside a young mother bouncing a fretful infant on her hip, the baby's face flushed with discomfort.

"Here she is now," Mr Henley said, gesturing toward Grace with undisguised pride. "Our Angel Grace will sort you right out."

Grace set down her basket and took the child gently. "Let's have a look at you, little one." She examined the swollen gums, noting the telltale signs of teething. "The yarrow tincture will help, but I'll add a touch of chamomile to help him sleep."

As she prepared the remedy, Mr Henley cleared his throat. "I've been meaning to speak with you, Grace. About your plans with Dr Coulson."

Grace looked up, measuring drops carefully into a small bottle.

"I've been thinking," he continued, polishing his spectacles with a handkerchief, "that perhaps we might consider a partnership. The three of us." He replaced his spectacles, blinking earnestly. "Your knowledge of herbs, Dr Coulson's medical training, my business sense and premises—together we could create something rather special."

Grace nearly dropped the bottle. "A partnership? Truly?"

"I'm not getting any younger," Mr Henley said with a self-deprecating smile. "And what you and Dr Coulson envision—a place where all might receive proper care regardless of means —it's something I've dreamed of myself." He gestured around the shop. "This could be just the beginning."

The bell above the door jingled, and Ronny strode in, his dock worker's frame filling the doorway. Though still lean, the past years had broadened his shoulders and strengthened his arms. He carried a small slate under one arm.

"Morning, Grace. Mr Henley." He nodded respectfully to both before turning to Grace with boyish enthusiasm. "Look here—I've been practising."

He held up the slate where he'd written in careful, if some-what wobbly, letters: *Edmund Coulson and Grace Hartwell.*

"Dr Coulson's been teaching me every evening after we finish at the dispensary," Ronny explained, pride evident in his voice. "Says I'm a quick study."

Mr Henley raised his eyebrows. "You're working with Dr Coulson now?"

"Started last week. Fetching supplies, keeping records— simple tasks, but he says I'll learn more as we go along." Ronny grinned. "Never thought I'd have proper employment, me who couldn't even write my own name a month ago."

The shop bell rang again as Mrs Demureson entered, carrying a basket covered with a cloth. "There you are, my dear. I've brought those fabric samples for your consideration." She set the basket on the counter, revealing swatches of cream and ivory silk. "For the wedding dress. Nothing too ostenta-tious, but befitting a respected healer."

Grace touched the fabrics reverently. "They're beautiful, but surely too fine for—"

"Nonsense," Mrs Demureson interrupted, her eyes twinkling. "Every bride deserves something special, particularly one who has worked as hard as you." She adjusted her shawl with a contented sigh. "I never had a daughter to fuss over, you know. You're indulging an old woman's dream."

Grace embraced her, throat tight with emotion. "You've been more than I could have hoped for."

Mrs Demureson patted her back. "The feeling is mutual, my dear."

The door opened once more, admitting Millicent Bashford —now Millicent Mercer—resplendent in a pale blue walking dress. "I hope I'm not interrupting," she said, her smile genuine. "Thomas is visiting parishioners, and I thought I might steal a moment with the bride-to-be."

"Millicent," Grace greeted her, still amazed by their unlikely friendship. "Not interrupting at all."

"I've come with news," Millicent said, eyes bright. "The children have been rehearsing diligently. Lizzie has a remarkable voice—she'll lead them in 'Amazing Grace' just as you requested."

"The street children?" Grace asked, her heart swelling.

"They're determined to make you proud," Millicent confirmed. "Even little Billy has memorised all the verses of your mother's favourite hymns."

Grace steadied herself against the counter, overwhelmed by the confluence of blessings. From Mr Henley's partnership offer to Ronny's new position, from Mrs Demureson's maternal affection to Millicent's friendship and the children's choir— each represented a thread in the tapestry of her new life.

"Are you quite all right, dear?" Mrs Demureson asked, concerned.

Grace nodded, blinking back tears. "Just grateful," she whispered. "So very grateful."

The young mother, who had been watching this parade of visitors with wide eyes, cradled her now-quieted baby. "Begging your pardon," she said softly to Grace, "but it seems you've built yourself quite a family."

Grace looked around at the faces surrounding her—each person once a stranger, now bound to her through love and respect.

"Yes," she agreed, her voice steady with certainty. "I have indeed."

63
FULL CIRCLE

Grace stood in the small antechamber of St Michael's Church, fingers trembling as she smoothed the cream silk of her wedding dress. Mrs Demureson had insisted on adding delicate embroidery along the modest neckline—tiny sprigs of yarrow and chamomile, herbs that had sustained Grace through her darkest days.

"You look beautiful," Mrs Demureson whispered, adjusting the simple veil. "Like an angel."

Grace touched the locket at her throat—her mother's portrait nestled inside—the one treasure she'd fought to keep through all her trials. "I wish they could be here," she murmured.

"They are, my dear." Mrs Demureson's eyes glistened. "In every kindness you've shown, in every life you've touched."

Through the door came the first notes of "Amazing Grace," sung by children's voices—clear and pure. Lizzie leading them just as Millicent had promised. The sound transported Grace back to the abandoned warehouse where she'd first gathered the street children, teaching them hymns from memory when her prayer book had been too damaged to read.

The church door opened, and Ronny appeared, dressed in a new suit that made him look suddenly grown.

"It's time," he said, offering his arm with uncharacteristic formality. "Unless you've changed your mind?" His teasing smile couldn't quite hide his pride.

Grace smiled, taking his arm.

The church doors opened fully, revealing pews filled with faces from every chapter of her life. Street vendors from the market stood beside ladies in fine hats. Dr Morrison beamed from the front row. Mr Henley nodded encouragingly. The street children, scrubbed clean but still unmistakably themselves, formed a small choir near the altar.

And there at the front stood Edmund, his face alight with joy.

As Grace walked down the aisle on Ronny's arm, she caught glimpses of her journey in the faces she passed. Martha from the match factory, now recovered from phosphorus poisoning. Old Maggie, whose persistent cough had finally cleared. The baker who'd once been her landlord. Even the constable who'd warned her about treating patients without a license nodded respectfully.

At the altar, Dr Reginald Coulson stood beside his son. When Grace reached them, the elder Dr Coulson stepped forward and took her hand from Ronny's, then placed it in Edmund's with deliberate ceremony.

"I welcome you, Grace Hartwell, to our family," he said, his voice carrying through the church. "Your compassion and wisdom have taught us all what true healing means."

Edmund squeezed her hand, his eyes never leaving hers as they turned toward Reverend Mercer—Millicent's husband— who waited to perform the ceremony.

"Dearly beloved," he began, "we are gathered here today ..."

Grace heard the familiar words as if in a dream, this sacred moment connecting past and present. She stood in the same church where her father had once prayed, surrounded by people from every walk of life—the wealthy and the destitute, the educated and the unschooled—all equal in this place of worship, just as they would be in the healing rooms she and Edmund would establish.

When the time came to speak her vows, Grace's voice rang clear and true. The light streaming through stained glass windows created patterns across the stone floor, reminding her of how her father had once brought light to London's darkest corners.

Now it was her turn to carry that light forward.

64
EIGHT YEARS LATER

Grace tucked the blanket around her youngest child, three-year-old Mary, who had finally surrendered to sleep after a third bedtime story. Beside her, five-year-old William and seven-year-old Emmeline lay curled together like kittens, their breathing soft and rhythmic in the lamplight.

"Was Grandfather really the best lamplighter in all of London?" Emmeline had asked earlier, her eyes wide with wonder.

"The very best," Grace had answered, smoothing her daughter's fiery curls. "He knew every street and alley. Even in the thickest fog, he could find his way."

Now, as Grace watched her children sleep, her heart swelled with gratitude. The small bedroom adjoined their living quarters above the Hartwell-Coulson Healing Rooms—the clinic she and Edmund had established five years earlier after their wedding. What had begun as a modest practice had blossomed into one of London's most innovative medical facilities, where the poor received the same quality of care as the wealthy.

Grace rose quietly and moved to the window. Below, gas lamps illuminated the evening streets, each globe of light a reminder of her father. She touched the locket at her throat—her mother's portrait still nestled inside—a talisman that had seen her through the darkest times.

"They're finally asleep, then?" Edmund's voice came softly from the doorway.

"Mary wanted the lamplighter story again," Grace said, turning to her husband with a smile. "She's as stubborn as her father."

"Hardly." Edmund crossed the room and slipped his arm around her waist. "I'd say she takes after her mother in that regard."

Downstairs, the last patient had departed an hour ago. The day had been particularly busy—three births, a broken arm, and numerous consultations. Yet Grace felt energised rather than exhausted. Every person who walked through their doors vindicated the dream she and Edmund had shared during those first days at St Bartholomew's Mission.

"Father is coming for dinner tomorrow," Edmund said, leading Grace from the children's room. "He wants to share the news about Bryant and May's reforms."

Grace nodded, still marvelling at how Dr Reginald Coulson had transformed from her fiercest opponent to one of her strongest advocates. After recovering from cholera under Grace's care, he had become passionate about improving conditions for factory workers, particularly at the match factory where Grace had once laboured.

"The new ventilation systems are installed," Edmund continued. "And they've finally replaced the white phosphorus with the safer red variety."

"Martha will be pleased," Grace said, thinking of her

former colleague who now served on the workers' committee. "She's fought so hard for those changes."

In the sitting room, Mrs Demureson sat knitting by the fire, her silver hair gleaming in the lamplight. The elderly woman had sold her house three years ago to move in with them, becoming the grandmother figure Grace had never known and the children adored.

"The little ones are settled, then?" Mrs Demureson asked, setting aside her knitting.

"Finally," Grace confirmed. "Though Mary extracted three stories before surrendering."

"That child could negotiate with Parliament," Mrs Demureson chuckled. "Oh, before I forget—Ronny's Sarah came by with an invitation to their anniversary supper next week."

Grace smiled at the mention of Ronny—once a scrawny street boy, now Edmund's skilled medical assistant—and his wife Sarah, one of the girls from Grace's warehouse congregation. Their marriage three years ago had been a joyous occasion, second only to the birth of their son last winter.

"I'll respond tomorrow," Grace promised, gathering her shawl. "But first, I need some air."

Edmund understood without words. "Take the lantern," he said, kissing her cheek. "It's getting dark."

Outside, the evening air carried the first hints of autumn. Grace walked with purpose, the lantern swinging gently in her hand as she followed the familiar route her father had walked for years. Each corner held memories—here where William had shown her how to light the lamps, there where he'd tended Mrs O'Malley's sprained ankle.

The streets had changed, yet remained the same. Children still played in doorways, women still gossiped at windows, men still trudged home from long days of labour. But now, many nodded to Grace with recognition and respect.

"Evening, Mrs Coulson," called a woman sweeping her step. "My Georgie's cough is much better with that syrup."

"Glad to hear it, Mrs Porter," Grace replied. "Send him round if it returns."

At the corner of Bell Street and Campton Lane, Grace paused. This was where her father had last set out into the fog, where Edmund had proposed, where her past and future had intertwined. She raised her lantern higher, its glow pushing back the gathering darkness.

Tomorrow would bring new patients, new challenges, and new opportunities to heal. But tonight, Grace simply stood in the light, carrying forward her father's legacy in her own way —bringing illumination not with gas and flame, but with knowledge, compassion, and love.

THE FIRST CHAPTER OF 'THE LOST ORPHAN OF THE PARISH'

Spring bloomed across St Michael's parish with shameless exuberance. Birdsong filled the air like scattered prayers, and the scent of wildflowers drifted through open windows. Ten-year-old Annabelle Sinclair sat leaning on the sill of her bedroom window, watching a robin hop around on the freshly turned soil. The world seemed determined to celebrate life while inside the house, everything whispered of its fragility.

Annabelle tucked a wayward copper curl behind her ear.

Her hair—"just like your mother's," everyone said—refused to stay confined, much like her thoughts. She traced a finger along the rough stone, feeling its cool solidity beneath her touch.

The vicarage had always been a place of warmth. Sunlight still streamed through the windows, illuminating the same furniture, the same books, the same worn Bible on the side table. Yet something had shifted. The rooms that once bubbled with laughter now held only echoes.

Mother's embroidery hoop sat abandoned in her favourite chair, the needle frozen mid-stitch in a half-finished garden scene. Father's theological texts remained scattered across his desk, pages marked with notes in his careful script. The spaces between these abandoned projects felt heavier than the objects themselves.

Annabelle rose and moved to the parlour window. Her reflection stared back—earnest blue eyes that Father claimed held wisdom beyond her ten years. She never quite understood what he meant by that, only that when she asked difficult questions about God or heaven, he would smile and say, "Those eyes of yours see right through to the heart of things."

Through the glass, she spotted her mother sitting in the garden alcove. Susan Sinclair's thin shoulders were wrapped in her woollen shawl despite the mild day. Her hand rose to her mouth as a cough shook her frame—gentle at first, then more insistent. The sunlight caught her profile, highlighting how sharp her features had become, how pale her skin against the vibrant spring colours.

Father appeared at Mother's side, his tall figure bending solicitously as he offered a handkerchief. Annabelle watched his face—the worry lines deepening around his eyes, the forced smile that didn't quite reach them. His hand lingered on

Mother's shoulder longer than usual, as if he could somehow transfer his strength to her through touch alone.

A knot formed in Annabelle's stomach, tight and uncomfortable. Something in Father's careful movements, in Mother's fragile posture, spoke of a truth no one had put into words.

Annabelle looked away from the window, drawing a deep breath. She slipped through the back door and crossed the garden path, her footsteps silent on the smooth stones. Mother's eyes brightened as she approached, and Father squeezed Mother's shoulder before excusing himself to prepare for Sunday's sermon.

"Come sit with me, my darling," Mother said, patting the stone bench beside her.

Annabelle settled next to her mother, careful not to jostle her. The bench felt cool through her cotton dress, but Mother's presence radiated a different kind of warmth.

"Your hair is wild today," Mother said, her voice thin but affectionate. She reached out with pale fingers to brush the unruly curls from Annabelle's forehead. "Just like mine was at your age. My mother used to say it was because I had too many thoughts trying to escape all at once."

Annabelle leaned into her mother's touch. "Do you think that's true?"

"Perhaps." Mother's fingers continued their gentle exploration, tucking strands behind Annabelle's ear. "Do you remember the stories I used to tell you about the girl with copper hair who could speak to birds?"

"She lived in a cottage at the edge of a great forest," Annabelle continued, the familiar tale flowing easily, "and every morning, the birds would bring her news from distant lands."

Mother smiled, her green eyes crinkling at the corners. "You always loved that one. You'd ask for it night after night."

"You never seemed to mind telling it."

"That's what mothers do—we tell the same stories over and over because they bring joy." Her hand stilled in Annabelle's hair. "And because we hope the lessons in them will stay with you long after the stories end."

Annabelle reached for her father's Bible that she'd brought outside with her. Its leather cover was smooth from years of handling, the pages well-thumbed and marked with ribbon. She traced the gold lettering on its spine.

"You taught me that faith isn't just about the grand miracles," Annabelle said quietly. "It's about finding God in small moments—like birds bringing messages or stories told over and over."

Mother's eyes glistened. "You listen so carefully. That's your gift, Annabelle." She took a laboured breath. "Remember that God speaks to us in whispers as often as in thunder. Sometimes His greatest strength shows in how we face our hardest days."

**Click here to read the rest of
'The Lost Orphan of the Parish'**

A tale of faith, loyalty, and the triumph of truth.

ANNABELLE SINCLAIR's world shatters when illness claims her beloved parents. Left alone at ten years old with no inheritance, she's sent to the harsh Thornfield Orphanage with nothing but her father's worn Bible and the memories of his gentle teachings.

Years later, a daring escape offers Annabelle a chance at a new life. Finding refuge in Meadowbrook village under a false identity, she becomes assistant to the village schoolmistress, where her natural teaching abilities begin to shine.

When the earnest new vicar, Edward Woolworth, arrives in the parish, Annabelle faces an impossible choice. Their shared passion for faith and education creates a powerful connection, but her secrets stand between them. As shadows from her past threaten to expose her true identity, a visiting church dignitary brings unexpected complications that could either destroy Annabelle's carefully constructed life or help reclaim something precious that was stolen from her family.

With the help of an old friend and her own courage, Annabelle must decide whether to keep hiding or take a stand that could cost her everything. Will her father's legacy and her own faith be enough to face the powerful forces aligned against her?

Follow Annabelle's journey from desperate circumstances to the heart of Meadowbrook parish in this unforgettable story of a young woman who discovers that faith flourishes most brilliantly in the darkest of times!

'The Lost Orphan of the Parish'

OUR GIFT TO YOU

AS A WAY TO SAY THANK YOU WE WOULD LOVE TO SEND YOU THIS BEAUTIFUL STORY FREE OF CHARGE.

Click here for your FREE COPY of

'The Little Orphan Waif's Crusade'

CornerstoneTales.com/sign-up

In the wake of her father's passing, seven-year-old Matilda is determined to heal her sister Effie's shattered spirit.

Desperate to restore joy to Effie's life, Matilda embarks on a daring quest, aided by the gentle-hearted postman, Philip. Together, they weave a plan to ignite the flame of love in Effie's heart once more.

At Cornerstone Tales we publish books you can trust. Great tales without sex or swearing, but with all of the mystery and romance you expect from a great story.

Be the first to know when we release new books, take part in our fun competitions, and get surprise free books in your inbox by signing up to our free VIP Reader list.

As a thank you you'll receive a copy of 'The Little Orphan Waif's Crusade' by *Rachel Downing* straight away, alongside other gifts.

Click here to sign up for our mailing list, and receive your FREE stories.

CornerstoneTales.com/sign-up

LOVE VICTORIAN ROMANCE?

More Dorothy Welling's Victorian Romance

The Moral Maid's Unjust Trial

Matilda must fend for herself when her father is wrongfully accused for a crime he didn't commit.

Get 'The Moral Maid's Unjust Trial' Here!

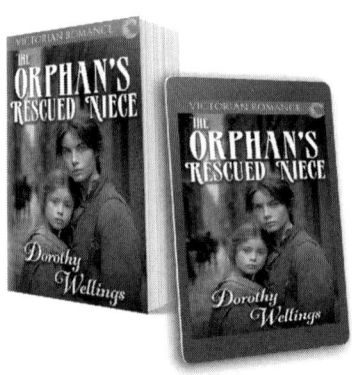

The Orphan's Rescued Niece

*As Beatrice grows from a wide-eyed child into a resilient young woman,
she finds herself caught between her love for her troubled brother and her
desire for a life free from poverty and fear.*

Get 'The Orphan's Rescued Niece' Here!

The Bookbinder's Orphan Daughter

Meredith's world crumbles when consumption claims her beloved mother and skilled bookbinder father. When a desperate attempt to find shelter leads her to break into a prestigious house, her life takes an unexpected turn.

Get 'The Bookbinder's Orphan Daughter' Here!

The Lost Orphan of the Parish

Annabelle Sinclair's world shatters when illness claims her beloved parents. Left alone at ten years old with no inheritance, she's sent to the harsh Thornfield Orphanage with nothing but her father's worn Bible and the memories of his gentle teachings.

Get 'The Lost Orphan of the Parish' Here!

Books by our other Victorian Romance Writer *RACHEL DOWNING*

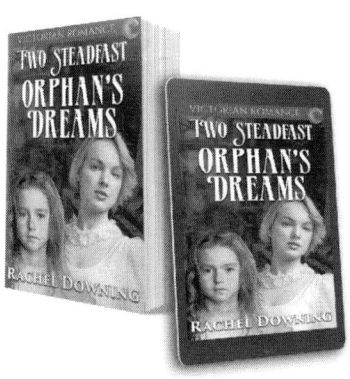

Two Steadfast Orphan's Dreams

Follow the stories of Isabella and Ada as they overcome all odds and find love.

Get 'Two Steadfast Orphan's Dreams' Here!

The Lost Orphans of Dark Streets

Follow the stories of Elizabeth and Molly as they negotiate the dangerous slums and find their place in the world.

Get 'The Lost Orphans of Dark Streets' Here!

The Orphan Prodigy's Stolen Tale

When ten-year-old Isabella Farmerson's world shatters with the tragic loss of her parents, she's thrust into a life of hardship and uncertainty.

Get 'The Orphan Prodigy's Stolen Tale' Here!

The Workhouse Orphan Rivals

Childhood sweethearts torn apart. A promise broken. A love that refuses to die.

Get 'The Workhouse Orphan Rivals' Here!

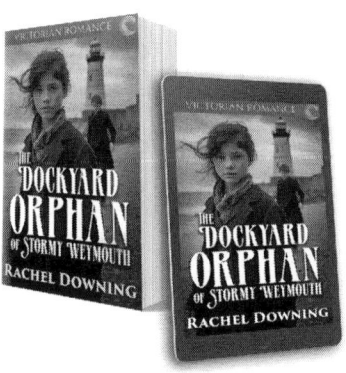

The Dockyard Orphan of Stormy Weymouth

Sarah Campbell's world crumbles when a tragic accident claims her parents' lives. She finds solace in the lighthouse's beam that guides ships to safety. But it's a young fisherman wrestling with his own loss, who truly captures her heart.

Get 'The Dockyard Orphan of Stormy Weymouth' Here!

The Orphan's Christmas Hymn

Seven-year-old Clara Winters' world shatters when tragedy strikes days before Christmas. Sent to St. Mary's Church Orphanage, she finds her only solace in the hymns that once filled her happy home. When her angelic voice catches the attention of the kind-hearted Reverend Thornton and his musically gifted son Edward, Clara dares to dream of a brighter future.

Get 'The Orphan's Christmas Hymn' Here!

The Workhouse Orphan's Redemption

In the brutal world of Victorian London, Emma Redbrook's life begins in tragedy. Orphaned and trapped in Grimshaw's Workhouse, she endures cruelty that would break most spirits. But Emma's unwavering faith becomes her beacon of hope — and her strength.

Get 'The Workhouse Orphan's Redemption' Here!

The Forsaken Lacemaker of Hampstead

Mabel Fairchild's life is shattered by false accusations and devastating loss. With two younger siblings dependent on her care, she makes an impossible promise: to keep her family together despite the world's cruel intentions.

Get 'The Forsaken Lacemaker of Hampstead' Here!

The Orphan's Letters to Providence

In the windswept Yorkshire countryside, Alice Wells's world shatters when tragedy strikes her beloved parents. Orphaned and thrust into a hostile household, she clings to his dying words: "Write to Providence, dear heart."

Get 'The Orphan's Letters to Providence' Here!

If you enjoyed this story, sign up to our mailing list to be the first to hear about our new releases and any sales and deals we have.

We also want to offer you a Victorian Romance novella - 'The Little Orphan Waif's Crusade' - absolutely free!

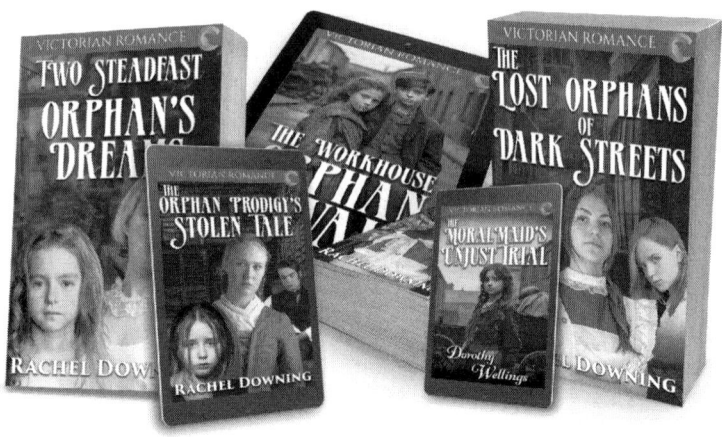

Click here to sign up for our mailing list, and receive your FREE stories.

CornerstoneTales.com/sign-up

Printed in Dunstable, United Kingdom